COMEBACK

CANTERWOOD CREST

COMEBACK

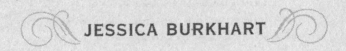 JESSICA BURKHART

ALADDIN M!X

New York London Toronto Sydney New Delhi

ALADDIN M!X

Simon & Schuster Children's Publishing Division

1230 Avenue of the Americas, New York, NY 10020

First Aladdin M!X edition August 2012

Copyright © 2012 by Jessica Burkhart

All rights reserved, including the right of reproduction

in whole or in part in any form.

ALADDIN is a trademark of Simon & Schuster, Inc., and related logo

is a registered trademark of Simon & Schuster, Inc.

ALADDIN M!X and related logo are registered trademarks

of Simon & Schuster, Inc.

For information about special discounts for bulk purchases,

please contact Simon & Schuster Special Sales

at 1-866-506-1949 or business@simonandschuster.com.

The Simon & Schuster Speakers Bureau can bring authors to your live event.

For more information or to book an event contact

the Simon & Schuster Speakers Bureau at 1-866-248-3049

or visit our website at www.simonspeakers.com.

Designed by Jessica Handelman

The text of this book was set in Venetian 301 BT.

Manufactured in the United States of America 1013 OFF

2 4 6 8 10 9 7 5 3

Library of Congress Control Number 2012939453

ISBN 978-1-4424-1952-0

ISBN 978-1-4424-1953-7 (eBook)

For everyone who's ever had to

make a comeback

ACKNOWLEDGMENTS

Merci to everyone at Aladdin: Bethany Buck, Fiona Simpson, Alyson Heller, Mara Anastas, Jessica Handelman, Nicole Russo, Courtney Sanks, Stephanie Voros, Dawn Ryan, Carolyn Swerdloff, Russell Gordon, Karin Paprocki, Craig Adams, Katherine Devendorf, Alex Penfold, Venessa Williams, and everyone who touched this book.

Special hugs of gratitude to Fiona and Bethany for going above and beyond, and helping me on a personal level.

As always, thank you to Monica Stevenson for this beautiful cover photo. Hugs to the models who made the cover look *très chic*!

I heart all of you on Team Canterwood! A girl couldn't ask for better readers. I'm thankful for you every time I sit down to write. ☺

Thank you to the S&S sales team, who has been getting Canterwood into the hands of readers. Huge thanks to the bookstores that have embraced the series.

Thank you, Kate Angelella, for your *très parfait* edits. The extra help with Lauren's French and the words of encouragement kept me in front of the computer. Otherwise, I probably would have been off chasing unicorns. . . . And, hey, I didn't throw a lip gloss at you this time! *De rien.* ☺ *Je t'aime!*

Brianna Ahearn, the write-a-thons with you were awesome! I want to do them for all of our future projects.

Lauren Barnholdt, the text you sent while I was writing is STILL making me giggle. *That* is why you should switch to a BlackBerry!

Ross Angelella, okay, okay. I'm a J-Ran. I said it! There. It's in print.

Thanks to all of my friends who helped me finish this book. xx

ALL THE CARDS
ON THE TABLE

KHLOE AND I SAT ACROSS FROM EACH OTHER, not moving, as if we were horses unsure whether to bolt or fight. We'd locked eyes, and neither of us had said a word since I'd last spoken.

Below us, riders readied for their lessons. Lexa had told Mr. Conner that Khloe and I were "sick" and had to miss our lessons. We'd been sitting on the floor of the stable's loft, surrounded by hay bales, for what felt like forever. The overpowering scent of hay tickled my nose. I sneezed.

"Bless you," Khloe said.

"Thanks." I took a deep breath, closed my eyes, then looked at Khloe. She'd drawn her knees to her chest. "Lexa dragged us up here to talk. Knowing her, she'll bring us food and water and not let us down until we talk. We're pretty much captives."

"I'll agree with you on that *one* thing," Khloe said. "And I think you should start talking." She yanked her long blond hair into a ponytail. "You're the one who just accused *me* of something that wasn't true."

"Khloe! I heard you!" I shook my head. "Why would I make that up? I was outside the tack room door, and you and Drew were talking." Just *thinking* about what I'd over-heard minutes ago made my stomach ache.

"You were eavesdropping. Did you even consider for a second that you'd, oh, I don't know, *misheard*? I can't believe you would think I'd say something awful about you."

I rubbed my dry lips together. "Then what did you say?"

"I ran into Drew in the tack room. We said hi, and I asked him about Mr. Conner during your lessons. Specifically, about how Mr. Conner acts with you."

"Like if he gives me 'special treatment?'" I rolled my eyes.

"No," Khloe said sharply. "Like if Mr. Conner started treating you different since he learned that your secret's out. I wanted to make sure he wasn't pressuring you to do more than anyone else in class. I asked Drew because I was worried. I trust Mr. Conner, and I believed he was coaching you the same as he had been since your first lesson here, but I wanted to make sure."

I stared at Khloe, letting her words sink in. I'd been so blinded by my like for Drew that I'd jumped to a very, *very* wrong conclusion. I was embarrassed over what I'd done—it wasn't me. I didn't turn against my friends over a boy.

Even though Khloe still had a lot of explaining to do about other things, I'd been wrong about this instance. I was *so* never eavesdropping again.

"Oh, God. Oh, no. Khloe." I picked up a piece of hay and twisted it around my index finger until the stalk snapped. "I'm so sorry. I should have talked to you about that before assuming anything."

"It's okay," Khloe said, shaking her head. "You didn't hear what I really said."

"But I know you better than that. I shouldn't have freaked out and run to Lexa. There were so many things that happened between us recently, and I—"

Khloe smoothed the front of her navy tee. "Like what?" She sat up straighter, raising an eyebrow.

"Like you not telling me first about Zack, sleeping

over at Lexa's last night, not saying anything to your guy friends about me . . ."

I trailed off, watching her face. She'd scrunched her nose, and her lips were parted.

"Before I address *any* of that, I have some things too," Khloe said. It felt like tension was building all over again and we were about to get into another fight. "How about your dropping advanced history when it could have been *any* other class, and your Sweet Shoppe date with Drew?"

Oh, mon Dieu. We were going to be up here all day.

"I didn't know you had a problem with either of those! We talked about them."

"And *I* explained about Zack, haven't had a second to talk to you about the sleepover, and you don't know the situation with Michael and those guys."

A small headache started between my eyes. I'd been a student at Canterwood Crest for less than a month, and I was fighting with my roommate. Not a squabble over something small like leaving clothes all over the floor or not rinsing toothpaste out of the sink. But serious issues that obviously hadn't been addressed between us.

"I'm listening," I said, raising my chin.

"First, we talked about the Zack thing. Laur, you'd been up late so many days in a row and you were finally asleep when he texted me to ask me out. What I told you then is *true*. I texted Lexa on a whim, and she happened to be awake." Khloe took a breath. "It was so hard not to wake you up and tell you. But I wanted you to rest."

Khloe's expression looked so sincere. She looked like the Khloe Kinsella who'd taught me everything about Canterwood when I'd arrived. The Khloe Kinsella who was still teaching me things. The girl who'd given me a campus tour, introduced me to her friends, and accepted me when I'd finally told her about my accident at Red Oak.

"You told me that next day," I said. I let out a breath. "I just got . . . I don't know! I got my feelings hurt that I wasn't the first to know. If I'd been in your position, I wouldn't have woken me either, but I also would have wanted to tell *someone*. I should have believed you the first time."

Khloe shrugged. "I thought you had."

"And I thought you'd taken my word about Mr. Spellman's history class," I said. I tried to keep the bite out of my tone, but my words came out sharp. "I meant what I said—I dropped the advanced part because it was more work than any of my other classes. The chances of me having to transfer to another class are practically zero."

"I knew in my gut you were telling the truth." Khloe

sighed. "You had no reason to potentially drop a class that you and I share. I don't know why my brain went there."

"I wish we had every class together. If I'd had any other options, I would have changed another class. Promise."

Khloe rubbed her hands over her tan face. "Maybe I really have been watching too many soap operas."

"How are you supposed to star in one if you don't watch them?" I asked, giving her a small smile.

Khloe returned the smile. "True. If only there was a story line about roommates at boarding school. Maybe it would give me tips to be a better roomie."

"You're a great roommate, Khlo. We've obviously been having some . . . communication problems lately. There's no reason for us not to trust each other."

Khloe nodded slowly. "There's not." She stopped, and I could tell she wanted to say something else.

I knew what she couldn't say or didn't want to. "Except for Red Oak. Khloe, if you have issues trusting me after I kept Red Oak from you, I understand. Please tell me."

Khloe shook her head, her ponytail flying. "This has nothing to do with Red Oak. Lauren, I promise, when you told me and everyone else about it—I asked questions, and if there was anything bothering me or something I wanted to know I'd have asked you."

We looked at each other for a few seconds before I answered. "Okay. Because I want you to trust me and believe me that my secret was a one-time thing. I hope it doesn't cloud the person you see now or how you trusted me before."

"It doesn't," Khloe said. "I think we had a lot going on and we took the easy way out—we got all caught up in our heads and went to Lexa. We know better—I should have come to you and not let all these things build."

"You're absolutely right. It shouldn't have taken Lexa to haul us up here to have this talk. You and I are more mature than that. And poor Lex. We both put her in a bad spot."

"Lexa didn't deserve it." Khloe tossed her head back, letting it bounce against a hay bale. "Speaking of Lex . . . Laur, I wasn't sleeping at her place. I was at Clare's. Riley left last night for her audition in New York City. Clare asked me last minute to sleep over. We never get to hang out without Riley, so I said yes."

Eavesdropping and assumptions had made me two for two in the wrong department. Major fail.

"I just assumed you were at Lexa's," I said. "That you didn't want to sleep in our room because you felt things were weird too."

Khloe's blue eyes stayed on my face. "Not at all! I'm

sorry about Clare's. It wasn't very roommate-like of me not to tell you that I was staying over when she asked me. It had to hurt your feelings to think I was at Lexa's."

"I respect your and Lexa's friendship outside of ours," I said. "If you had been staying with her, I wouldn't have cared. It bothered me that I didn't find out until later that you were staying out."

"I get it," Khloe said. "I'd feel exactly the same way. Just like I would have felt like you did with my guy friends."

Every single thing we laid out on the table felt good. We moved forward with each confession.

"If I'd come to a new school," Khloe continued, "and a bunch of guys I didn't know but seemed to know you very well descended on our lunch table, it would have been so weird. I would have been like, 'Dude, who *are* all of you, and why do you know my BFFL LT but not me?'"

Khloe's theatrics made me smile.

"Those guys aren't my close friends," she said. "They're people I share classes with and have run into around campus. The beginning of this year has been so crazy, I hadn't said more than 'hi' to any of them. You're so cool with everyone that I shouldn't have assumed you'd be fine and left you with them."

I sagged back into the hay bale. Everything I'd doubted

about Khloe seemed neurotic now. How had so many misunderstandings been possible? "I get it now," I said. "I really do."

"If I'd had time to have a real conversation with them, I would have told them all about you. I wasn't hiding you—I promise."

"I went way overboard on that," I said. "Lexa even told me those guys weren't your best friends. Clearly, I have been influenced by your soap-opera ways." That made Khloe smile. "I let my imagination go crazy. *Bad* crazy. Like, I thought you were swapping places part-time with your twin, like on *Pretty in Port Royal*. I'm sorry."

"If only I had a twin," Khloe said, cracking a grin. "I don't think I've ever said 'I'm sorry' or heard 'I'm sorry' so much in such a short time."

"Me either. But you're going to have to hear it again, because I want to explain about—"

Khloe held up her hands, palms facing me. "I think we've apologized to each other enough. You agree?"

"Definitely. Unless there's something—anything—else you want to ask me. I don't want you to walk away from this with any questions or lingering doubts."

Khloe scooted closer, closing the giant gap between us. "I don't have any. I promise. Do you?"

Relief replaced the dread that had pumped through me. "I don't. I think there are two things left to do. First thing: I want to promise that if I ever feel something's off or think you're mad at me or whatever, I'll ask you instead of dreaming up scenarios gone so, so wrong. I hope you'll do the same."

"I swear," Khloe said. "If you wake up and I see your eyebrow twitch in a weird way, I'll be like, 'LT, what's up? Is something wrong? Are you harboring a deep, dark secret from me?'"

We giggled.

"Definitely watch out for my eyebrows." I wiggled both of them.

Khloe laughed, and we both reached out our arms to each other. We hugged, and I silently vowed never to let things get so out of control with any of my friends.

We let go of each other, smiling, and Khloe sat beside me. "I bet I can guess the second thing," she said. "Lexa."

"Yeah. I owe her a huge apology. It's okay to ask friends for advice, but not like I did with Lex. It's a miracle she didn't lock me in a stall or something!"

"Same. I used our friendship for the wrong reason, and Lexa deserves better than that. After all we put her through, Lex still cared enough to bring you and me up here and make sure we talked things out."

I stood, then offered a hand to Khloe and pulled her up. "It definitely took one very wise Lexa Reed to make us do what we needed to."

"I hope you spent the last hour talking about each other and not me," a voice said. Lexa appeared around a stack of hay bales. Her boots had a fine coat of arena dust, and there were a few red and white horsehairs on her shirt. She glanced between Khloe and me like she was trying to figure out if we'd made up or not.

"We only said awesome stuff about you," Khloe said. "Lauren and I worked out everything because you forced us up to this hay dungeon."

Lexa cocked a hip, smiling.

I nodded. "Everything we thought was wrong. All these little misunderstandings kept adding up and made us—"

"Insane," Khloe finished. "Lex, I'm so, so sorry. I didn't act like your best friend when I came to you with my worries about Lauren."

"I'm sorry, too, Lexa," I said. "All the questions I asked you were things I should have asked Khloe."

Lexa ran a hand over her curly black hair. "Apologies accepted. You guys care about each other, and it came across—in the wrong way—when you kept asking me questions about the other."

"So, you're not mad?" Khloe asked, bouncing on her tiptoes.

Lexa smiled. "Nah. All I care about is that you two worked it out."

"Yay!" I said. "Thanks, Lex!"

We three-way hugged. All my worries and insecurities about Khloe melted as I squeezed my friends.

"There is *one* thing," Lexa said when we stepped back.

"Name it," Khloe said.

"Totally yours," I said.

"The Sweet Shoppe has a new triple-layer chocolate cake that I'm dying to try," Lexa said.

Khloe and I smiled. "Deal!" we said simultaneously.

2

I'M IN

FRIDAY CLASSES ALWAYS WENT ONE OF TWO ways: Time either crawled by, or I barely had time to catch my breath between courses and didn't have time to wish for the weekend to come sooner.

Today's classes went the second way. I dashed from building to building, collecting stacks of homework, raising my hand in class, smiling at people in the hallway, and finally taking a seat in study hall. Last class of the day.

I opened my Chatter application and typed a message. *LaurBell: Friday @ last! So xcited 4 my lesson w @Lexaaa, @ColeIam, @SwmerGuy, and @CutieClare.*

I didn't have to include Riley (*@OfficiallyRiley*), since she wasn't here. It had been a sort of freeing day—not having to worry about running into "Reiler" (Khloe's nickname for her) on campus or having to avoid eye contact with her during one of our shared classes. If it wouldn't upset Khloe so much, I wished Riley would get the part she was auditioning for in New York City. And *stay* there.

I posted the message, wondering if Drew would see it. I'd looked him up on Chatter last night and found his handle. It had taken me until now to come up with a good enough reason to Chat at him.

Mr. Davidson, my English teacher, was monitoring the period. He was engrossed in grading papers, so I slipped my BlackBerry out from my pocket and held it under my desk. I made sure it was on silent, then typed a BlackBerry Message to Khloe.

Lauren:

What do u think abt sleepover 2nite? U, me, Lex, Clare?

Seconds later, *Khloe is writing a message* appeared.

Khloe:

♥! Want me 2 ask Clare if we can go 2 her place? U haven't been there and neither has L.

Lauren:

Sounds perf. Let me know! ☺

I put my phone on my lap and opened my English folder. My class was still working on memoirs. Today Mr.

Davidson had assigned *I Know Why the Caged Bird Sings* by Maya Angelou. We had to read the first three chapters and pay attention for potential essay topics, listing them as we read. The syllabus said we had a paper due a couple of weeks after we finished the book.

My phone blinked. The pink smiley face on my phone screen meant I had a new mention.

BrielleisaBeauty: @LaurBell: Wish @AnaArtiste & I had a lesson w u! xx

Smiling, I typed back to Brielle, my Briar Creek bestie. *@BrielleisaBeauty: Miss u and @AnaArtiste 2! Skype soon! Say hi 2 Kim 4 me.* ☺

Another message came before I exited the app.

@LaurBell: Xcited abt r lesson. C u there. ☺

It was from Drew. Or, SwmerGuy. OMD! Should I write back? Or was this his reply to me, and then I'd be replying to a reply, which would be weird? I couldn't decide, so I exited Chatter and tried to focus on homework.

So far I'd only read a couple of pages and the handout Mr. D had given us. He'd warned us that the book was tough subject matter, but it was something he wanted to expose to our class. Apparently, it focused on African-American issues and women's rights.

Mom would be proud that I was learning about both

of those—especially women's rights. She always instilled her belief that women could do anything men could do upon my sisters and me. I smiled, thinking back to Take Your Kid to Work Day last year. Charlotte, my oldest sister, had been away at Sarah Lawrence College, but Becca and I had gotten the day off from Yates to go with Mom.

We'd dressed in skirts, fitted shirts and shiny ballet flats, and swapped our backpacks for purses. Mom had driven us to the law firm where she worked—an enormous steel-and-glass building. Becca and I had to check in at security, and the guard gave us badges with our photos on them. We'd ridden an elevator up ten stories to Mom's floor.

All day we watched her do lawyer stuff. She made lots of phone calls, paced back and forth in her stilettos, read piles of documents on her desk, and drank *lots* of coffee. She let Becca and me take turns playing secretary and answering her phone. We had to say, "Hello, you've reached the law office of Ms. Towers. How may I assist you?" Then we took messages. I'd thought the day would be (sorry, Mom!) boring, but it was cool to see her in action.

I opened my English notebook, started a new page for Ms. Angelou's book, and started reading. I'd read the first page when my phone blinked. I checked it and opened a BBM from Khloe.

Khloe:

Every1's in! C said we should def come 2 her room. Yay 4 2nite!

Lauren:

Awesome! V xcited! C u @ the stable.

Khloe:

I saw DREW Chattered @ u! :D

Lauren:

I know! Eeeek!

Khloe:

LOL. Awe-SOME!

I went back to my book, trying to focus on the text. Soon the words pulled me in, and I flipped the pages, forgetting to be thinking about an essay topic.

". . . dismissed and happy Friday!" Mr. Davidson's voice jolted me out of my reading. Everyone around me shoved back their chairs, piled textbooks into their bags, and rushed for the door. I hurried out with them—I wanted to get back to my room as fast as possible, change, and get to the stable.

Whisper. Thinking her name made me smile. I hadn't had a lot of free time to spend with her this week. I missed her even though we'd had a lesson every day except yesterday.

We needed some QT stat. Mr. Conner had told each of us on the seventh-grade intermediate team to meet outside the stable. My gut said one thing: cross-country.

Back in my room, I pushed aside my dirty laundry basket and opened my closet door. I'd already tossed down my backpack and kicked off my ankle boots. I reached for the stack of breeches and pulled out a moss-colored pair. I looked at my T-shirts, going through them twice. *Just pick one!* I said to myself. I yanked a black V-neck with white stitching off a hanger and got dressed.

I was glad Khloe hadn't witnessed that. She would have pointed out the exact reason why I was taking so long with a shirt for *lessons*. It might have had something to do with a certain black-haired, blue-eyed boy.

In the bathroom, I gathered my loose waves and pulled them into a low ponytail. I grabbed my makeup bag from under the sink and pulled out an oil-blotting sheet. I pressed it on my nose, chin, and forehead, then tossed it in our trash can. A coat of shiny gloss with SPF and I was ready. My pale skin looked stark against the T-shirt; my blue eyes were the focus of my face, since I'd kept everything else neutral; and my light-brown hair was smooth.

I grabbed my bag for the stable and left. Outside Hawthorne Hall, the September air was warm. I took my favorite route to the stable—skipping the main sidewalk and taking less populated ones to the giant black and white building.

Happiness bubbled inside me the closer I got. Horses always had that effect on me. I passed glossy fences that held beautiful horses inside. Several pastures, big and small, were separated by gates. Some horses grazed in herds, a few sipped water from the troughs, and a playful few chased one another, squealing and dancing when another horse got too close.

I laughed. There was something beautiful about seeing horses play and be free without any interaction from a person. Each horse had his or her own distinct personality, which really came through during playtime. But even during play, something was different about Canterwood horses. *These* horses could change from mischievous to competitive in seconds. Just like their riders. The dizzying variety of breeds—some bred for speed and others for strength— were always *on*. Watching the horses interact was almost like seeing riding students dance around one another.

Walking a bit faster, I stepped onto the gravel driveway in front of the stable and walked through the open double doors. The stable was packed for a Friday. No way was I going to find a pair of cross-ties. Horses and riders filled the main aisle, and the hot walker buzzed as horses followed the mechanical arm around the circular track. I stood on my tiptoes, but I didn't see Drew.

I took a left, going down a side aisle to the tack room. Unlike yesterday, when I'd hovered outside the door and eavesdropped on Drew and Khloe, I pushed open the door and walked right inside. The tack room was almost the size of my living room at home. Rows and rows of gleaming saddles lined the walls. Bridles hung above them on pegs. A colorful array of saddle pads were paired with each saddle. We couldn't use fun colors to show, but Mr. Conner allowed them for practice.

I reached Whisper's gear. I put my arm under her saddle, picked out a hot-pink saddle pad, and slid her bridle from the peg and onto my shoulder. Sometimes, it still didn't seem real that Whisper was *my* horse. After riding stable horses for my entire riding career, Whisper had been a gift from my parents for my acceptance to Canterwood.

Whisper and I were the newest pair on the intermediate team—we'd only been together since the summer. Imagining her sweet face made me hurry out of the tack room, down the side aisle, and back to Whisper's stall.

"Happy Friday, girly!" I said, putting her tack on top of her trunk.

A low whicker came from inside the box stall, and before I reached the door, Whisper stuck her head over and looked at me.

"Hi, beautiful." I put a hand on her baby-blue halter and used the other to scratch her cheek. Whisper, the lightest shade of gray I'd ever seen, was a Hanoverian-Thoroughbred mix. She had no markings except for the black and pink snip that I loved to kiss. "You ready for today's lesson?" I asked.

Whisper closed her eyes and lowered her head. When she opened her eyes, her flirty, curly lashes blinked at me. Liquid brown eyes looked sweet and full of understanding. Whisper was my dream horse, and I couldn't imagine Canterwood—or my life—without her. A lot of her past was a mystery to me, and sometimes I could sit for hours and imagine where she'd lived, who'd ridden her, and how we'd ended up together.

I unlatched the stall door and lightly put my hand on Whisper's chest to move her back. I pulled a matching lead line off the hook at the stall door and went inside. Whisper sniffed my hands and arms, tickling me with her whiskers, as I clipped the lead line to her halter.

"Not yet, missy," I said, grinning at her. I tied her to the iron bars at the front of her stall. "You get treats *after* our lesson. Not before."

Whisper gave up and let out a short sigh, disappointed.

"I think you'll make it *just* fine," I said.

I stepped outside her stall, then moved her tack to get into my wooden trunk for her grooming kit.

"Oh, hey!" I said, looking up to see Lexa. Her mare, Honor, was Whisper's neighbor.

"Crazy busy, right?" Lexa asked. She had a purple lead line in her hands. "I'm copying you and doing the stall grooming and tacking up too."

"Yeah, it's not even worth trying to find a pair of cross-ties. Let me know when you're done if you finish first, and we can go to the arena together."

Lexa nodded.

We split into our stalls and got to work, in too much of a hurry to talk. I hung Whisper's grooming kit on her stall door and fished out her hoof pick. Starting with her right front hoof, I used the metal to pry loose layers of dirt. I ran the metal all along the shoe's inside, checking for pebbles. I released her clean hoof and patted her side as I moved to one hind leg. She lifted it when I ran my hand down her leg, pressed my body slightly against her, and squeezed above her hoof. After picking this hoof, I peered at the shoe, frowning.

"I think it's time to ask Mr. Conner to schedule you

a visit from the farrier," I said. "This shoe's growing off faster than the front."

The rest of her shoes and hooves were fine, but I made a mental note to talk to Mr. Conner after our lesson. When I recalled when she'd last been shod, I realized that Whisper was due for a new set of shiny shoes.

Whisper treated grooming like a princess getting pampered. She made tiny grunts as I worked the body brush through her near-white coat. "Good girl," I said. "No stains!" Keeping her gorgeous coat clean wasn't easy. Her mane and tail took minutes—the wide-toothed plastic comb ran through the strands.

I'd braid her tail and give her mane button braids for the schooling show. Thinking about it made me shiver. The show was only two weeks away.

Stop obsessing! Go back to thinking about braiding, I told myself.

I liked using a needle and thread and making the bunlike plaits that showed off my horse's neck whenever I competed. "It'll be the first time I'm braiding *you*," I said to Whisper.

"Tacking up!" Lexa's voice carried over the stall wall.

"Me too!"

I grabbed a clean cloth and ran it over Whisper's

muzzle and eye area, then picked up her tack from outside the stall. I lifted my Butet saddle onto her back and lowered it onto the clean saddle pad. I tightened her girth and moved to her head. After slipping off her halter, I put the bit in the palm of my hand and raised the bridle over her head. She took the snaffle bit without pause, chomping on it for a second while I bucked the straps. A recheck of her girth and we were set.

I grasped the rubber-grip reins I loved using during lessons. The rainbow reins were perfect for practice, especially jumping. They kept my fingers from sliding, and I didn't need gloves.

Lexa and I met outside our horses' stalls. Whisper's ears swiveled as she listened to the sounds of other horses and riders around her. Honor, seemingly uninterested, kept her head near Lexa's arm, her body relaxed. The strawberry roan was beyond used to the noise of the stable.

"Let's go," Lexa said.

We strapped on our Lexington helmets and maneuvered our horses through the busy aisle. Outside, puffy clouds muted the sunlight, and the air was warm but not hot.

Cole, another rider on our team, was waiting and mounted on his black gelding, Valentino.

"Hey," he said to Lexa and me. "Friday! Finally, right?"

"If I had *one* more class, my brain would explode," Lexa said, halting Honor.

"Same," I said. Whisper stopped beside Honor, and I swung myself into her saddle. "You doing anything fun tonight, Cole?"

He nodded, grinning. "Going with a group of guys to see the new slasher flick at the media center. This week at school was scarier than anything I'm going to see on the screen."

We laughed.

"We're sleeping over at Clare's," Lexa said. "Since Her Highness, aka Riley, is away, we're actually allowed to hang with Clare and visit her room. Khloe's coming, too."

Cole patted Valentino's neck, looking up at us with teasing bright green eyes. "Aw, you girls are going to paint your nails, braid each other's hair, and have a pillow fight."

"Totally," I said. "Don't forget the pints of Ben & Jerry's we're going to eat."

Hoofbeats struck the gravel, and Clare, followed closely by Drew, headed for us. They greeted us and both mounted. I tried not to look-slash-stare at Drew immediately.

"Did I hear someone say something about Ben & Jerry's?" Drew asked.

Okay, now that he'd spoken, that made it legit for me

to look at him. I glanced over at him. We'd formed an irregular kind of semicircle in the yard.

Drew looked *très parfait* on horseback. He sat tall on Polo, his blood bay gelding. His cropped black hair was hidden beneath his helmet, and his dark blue eyes stood out against his pale skin. A swimmer and a rider, Drew had an athletic body. He was in shape but didn't look as though he spent most of his life in the gym.

"Yeah," I said to him. "The girls and I plus Khloe are sleeping at Clare's tonight. We're going to raid the freezer for anything with chocolate, sprinkles, caramel. You know, anything of the ice cream variety."

Drew and Cole shot each other glances. "What if one of *us* wants ice cream?" Drew asked, tilting his head and smiling.

"You're really going to leave us frozen-dairy-less?" Cole asked, mock-wide-eyed.

"We are," Clare said, grinning. "But maybe we can be persuaded to leave you guys *something*."

"Girls versus guys?" Lexa asked. "Whichever team does better during today's lesson wins first shot at the freezer."

The girls looked at each other, but I stared at Whisper's mane. I reached for my throat and played with my neck-lace. The beryl birthstone necklace my parents had gotten me for my birthday was one of my fave pieces of jewelry. I always rubbed the pool-blue necklace when I was anxious. We were doing cross-country. There was no way I'd be better than Cole or Drew.

"Um, the numbers are unfair," I interjected. "There are three of us and two of them." I grasped my necklace, hoping my observation would get me out of the competition. "I'm totally willing to play but not be judged. Then it's two on two."

"No way," Clare said, shaking her head. "Please." She looked at Cole and Drew. "You guys threatened by another rider on our team?"

Drew's eyes met mine. There was a flicker of *something*.

He smiled at us. "I'm totally cool with three against two. But if Lauren doesn't think it's fair and wants to sit out, she should."

Cole, catching on, nodded. "I agree. Totally up to you, Laur. We'll either take you *all* down or you can watch Drew and me decimate your friends."

I couldn't help laughing when he said "decimate." Cole was the nicest, sweetest guy and the least likely among all of us to "decimate" anyone.

I let go of my necklace, glancing at Drew. "Well, when Cole puts it *that* way . . . I can't let my team be destroyed without me. I'm in."

Drew smiled, and Lexa and Clare whispered to each other. I'd made the right decision. I was done backing down.

"Who's judging?" I asked.

That made us pause. Boots crunched in the gravel, and the five of us looked up at our answer.

3

BOYS VS. GIRLS

"GOOD AFTERNOON, CLASS," MR. CONNER said.

The tall, dark-haired instructor was dressed in a crisp white polo and black breeches. He carried his usual clipboard, and a pen peeked out of his shirt pocket.

"Good afternoon, Mr. Conner," we replied.

"I asked you all to meet me here so we could head out to the cross-country course together. It's an area I want to spend time on with each of you today. We will not be doing any of the more advanced courses."

Whew.

"The goal will be to tackle the obstacles in front of you with well-timed approaches, clean landings, and within the time I designate for you to finish the course."

I kept my eyes on Mr. Conner, trying to ignore my pounding heart. I wished I could make Pepto-Bismol appear in front of me. The idea of cross-country was making me a little nauseous. I reached down, rubbing a hand on Whisper's shoulder. The mare didn't seem nervous at all, thankfully. Instead, she seemed happy to be outside—her eyes were wide, she flicked her ears at the tweets of the birds, and she felt relaxed beneath me.

Lexa raised her hand, a mischievous smile on her face. "Mr. Conner? We were talking before you came, and we wondered if you'd help us with something. It would up our riding game."

Mr. Conner squinted, looking curious. "How can I help?"

"Would you play 'judge' during our lesson?" Lexa asked. Honor swiveled her ears at the sound of her owner's voice. "Pretend we're two teams—boys versus girls. At the end of the lesson, whatever team you think did the best wins."

Mr. Conner smiled. "Usually I'd say no, because I want you to focus on working together and as a team. Plus, this *is* practice, not a competition. That said, I like that you're in the competitive mood." He nodded. "Do your best, ladies and gentlemen. I'll reveal my decision at the end of class."

"Thanks, Mr. Conner!" Cole said. The rest of us chimed

in our thanks. My earlier nerves melted a little when I looked at my teammates. I was happy to play along with everyone else, and I didn't want to leave Whisper out of anything.

"Let's head out to the main field to warm up, and then we'll discuss the jumps," Mr. Conner said.

We walked our horses down the side drive and to the large field. Our group gathered on one of the many hills of campus. I had the perfect view of campus from atop Whisper's back. I tried to pay attention to Mr. Conner, but my eyes darted to different places on campus.

The tennis court.

The outdoor pool.

The dorms—from Winchester to Orchard to Blackwell.

The tops of school buildings.

And the long, winding driveway, lined with dark fences and dotted with street lanterns, that led to the tree-lined entrance and exit of campus. Sometimes it was overwhelming that *I* was here.

"Lauren?"

I looked up, blinking at Mr. Conner.

"I'm sorry."

"Please pay attention," he said.

I nodded. I was glad Riley wasn't here to have witnessed that.

"Take about fifteen minutes to warm up," Mr. Conner said. "You don't need me to tell you how to warm up. Go ahead and get started—feel free to spread out, but stay within eyesight."

I squeezed my boots against Whisper's sides, and we staked out a section of the plain. Drew, Cole, Lexa, and Clare did the same. I put Whisper through a normal warm-up, enjoying the change of scenery. Whisper listened to every cue, and I was almost sorry when Mr. Conner raised his hand, signaling that time was up.

He explained the course—ten obstacles that were clearly marked with the usual red-and-white flags.

I looked over at Lexa on my right. *Okay?* she mouthed.

I nodded. I was.

Mostly.

"We're going to move to the middle of the course so you can watch each of your teammates," Mr. Conner said. "I'd like Clare to go first, then Drew, Lauren, Lexa, and Cole."

Clare smiled and settled into her saddle.

"Clare, head toward the first jump and begin when we've gathered out of the way. The rest of you, please follow me."

Fuego swished his cinnamon-colored tail as he and

Clare separated from our group. We headed in the opposite direction, and Mr. Conner stopped us in the center of the short course. From here, we could see almost every jump.

Clare circled Fuego in a large circle at a trot, then a canter. When they reached a solid canter, Clare pointed her gelding in a straight line at the first obstacle—a row of brush. The horse and rider, looking small from here, cleared the brush and cantered toward the second jump. It was another row of brush, but wider than the first.

Fuego took the jump and the pair moved closer, becoming easier to see by the second as they approached our waiting group. Clare was a focused rider. She didn't let anything get her attention away from her horse or their ride. Fuego was just as in tune with her—they tackled one jump after the other. Along with everyone else, I clapped when Clare finished and eased Fuego to a halt next to Polo.

"That was a great ride, Clare," Mr. Conner said. "There was a visible unity between horse and rider. Fuego took this course so well because of his deep trust in you. Continue working as a pair as you've been. I'm impressed."

"Thank you, sir," Clare said. Her smile was contagious.

Drew and Polo went next. I found myself gripping the reins, holding my breath, and standing in my stirrups during his ride. It was almost as if I was on course—I wanted him to do well. He guided his lanky blood bay over the course and made it look *so* easy. I tried not to clap like an overly caffeinated fan girl when he and Polo finished.

Drew stopped Polo, then pushed up his white helmet and patted the horse's shoulder. He flicked his eyes to me and I grinned, dropping the reins and giving him a thumbs-up. Drew's light skin was flushed from the exercise. He smiled back at me in a way that wasn't just *merci, Lauren!* but reached his eyes, too.

"Drew, that was a strong ride," Mr. Conner said. He glanced up from his clipboard. "You're a consistent rider. I can't stress enough how important that is both for you, as an individual rider, and for your team. When I prepare to watch you ride, I know what kind of ride to expect." Drew smiled. "You also continue to grow, and there are subtle, but notable, degrees of improvement in almost every cross-country ride of yours that I witness."

Drew tipped his head, then looked up. "Thank you, Mr. Conner. I really appreciate your comments, and I'll keep working hard."

Mr. Conner gave Drew a quick smile before turning to me. "Lauren, are you ready?"

I nodded. I was too afraid to speak in case my voice came out squeaky. Mr. Conner's brown eyes seemed to be trying to send a silent message of reassurance. Like he knew Whisper and I could do this. We had, too, in the time I'd been at Canterwood. But only a couple of jumps and not a full course.

Stop thinking! Go!

I tapped my boot heels against Whisper's sides, and raising her head high, she moved into a trot. If I wasn't ready, she definitely was. Her hoofbeats, muffled by the grass, were rhythmic and even.

We trotted away from our group, and I fought to find the place in my brain where Competition Lauren still existed. Competition Lauren could block out anything— from trash talkers on opposite teams to nerves over people having higher scores—and I needed to tap into her now.

I took a quick breath, settled my tailbone into the saddle, and asked Whisper for a canter. The ground was firm, but there were soft patches from the overnight rain. I crossed my fingers that no one before me had hit the same areas, churning up the grass and making a muddy mess.

Whisper switched gaits and had an ear back to me and an ear pointed forward. I took her through two large circles to warm up before pulling on the right rein and aligning her with the first jump. Brush was one of my favorites. When I was little, I had pretended that I was a steeplechaser and had raced ponies over any brush fences I could find. I'd even convinced Mom to sew me a pair of blue-and-white jockey silks.

The jump rushed at us, and I rose into the two-point position. Unlike me, Whisper hadn't been daydreaming. She propelled herself into the air at the right moment, and we easily cleared the brush.

One down! I couldn't help but smile.

Six strides later, I lifted my seat out of the saddle and Whisper jumped over the second hedge. She landed, hooves far away from touching the greenery, and snorted. She tossed her head, gray mane flying. Whisper deserved to feel good, but I had to keep her focused. As a young, green horse, she needed a rider who paid attention and kept her on track.

We'd settled into a rhythm by the time the third, fourth, and fifth jumps were behind us. Whisper hadn't batted a curly eyelash at the two red-and-white verticals or the oxer made out of logs.

I kept my hands steady as we reached thin fence boards. Mr. Conner had made the course safe—all the jumps were designed with material that would break or be knocked down if a horse didn't clear the obstacle. I rose into the air, and Whisper tucked her forelegs beneath her and propelled us over the jump with her strong hindquarters. Every muscle in her body was engaged—it made our ride feel *electric*.

I turned Whisper in a half circle and we started to canter up a slight incline. *Oops.* I started sliding backward in the saddle. The "slight incline" was a little steeper than I'd thought. Tightening my abs, I leaned forward and wrapped my fingers through Whisper's mane for extra support. She huffed, working hard. Her canter slowed a touch from earlier, and I let her so she didn't overexert herself. *Only a few more strides, girl!* I wanted to tell her. We reached the hilltop, and the field leveled out with the final jumps ahead of us.

We weren't *that* high up, but Mr. Conner and the other riders and horses looked small. It felt like a private session with Whisper, where we could focus on the final jumps without anyone watching us so closely.

Whisper took a vertical with bright yellow flowers in between the first and second pole. The ground turned a little soggier, and I slowed her before the next jump. Whisper snorted, tugging against the reins. She'd been having fun cantering at her own pace, but we had to be more careful on the potentially slippery terrain. One jump to go!

I sat deep in the saddle until the final seconds before the oxer and then lifted out of the saddle. Whisper's take-off was clean and she lifted into the air, her hooves making a slight suction-y sound against the grass.

We landed, and as I guided her away from the jump, readying to start our descent down, something felt *off*. One of her back hooves was striking the ground, but not making a sound like the others. Whisper's ears flicked back and forth; she was losing concentration because of whatever was going on.

Oh, no.

I eased her to a halt as fast as possible and dismounted. Mr. Conner was already making his way up the hill, while everyone else waited below.

I walked to Whisper's hindquarters and ran my hand down her left leg, squeezing above her fetlock. She offered me her hoof: bare.

"Lauren," Mr. Conner said. "What happened?"

I gently put down Whisper's hoof and turned to Mr. Conner, who was standing at her head and holding the reins.

"She threw a shoe," I said, trying to keep calm. "It's my fault. I looked at her hooves this afternoon and knew she was overdue for shoes. I should have asked to sit out when I realized we'd be riding over soft ground. I didn't even think about it."

Mr. Conner put a hand on my shoulder. "Lots of horses, though it's not healthy for their hooves, go a long, *long* time without having their shoes replaced. I checked all the charts for horses who needed shoes, and I already had Whisper down for this week."

"Thank you," I said, rubbing my forehead. "But she's always used to being shod. What if she bruised her hoof when she cantered without a shoe?"

"Let me take a look," Mr. Conner said. "I'm betting, though, that the softer ground played to your advantage today."

I took the reins from Mr. Conner and stood by Whisper's head. She was breathy from finishing the course, and I rubbed her cheek. Looking up into her amber eyes, I offered a silent apology.

It felt like an eternity had passed before Mr. Conner released Whisper's leg and faced me. I flicked my tongue over my permanent bottom retainer—nervous habit.

"I don't see any hint of bruising or trauma to the

hoof," he said, smiling. "You pulled her up the second you felt something was wrong. Had you kept going . . . well, we could be having a very different conversation."

I let out a giant breath. "I'm so glad she's okay."

Mr. Conner patted Whisper's neck and the gray, closing her eyes, leaned into his touch. "I'll make a note for the farrier to take an extra-close look at Whisper, but I don't foresee any different news."

I nodded. "Thank you again, Mr. Conner."

"Of course. Now, your lesson is over for today. Walk Whisper back to the stable and get her groomed. Go find one of the stable hands if you need help with anything until I'm finished here."

Mr. Conner started back to the awaiting group, and I led Whisper downhill. I'd been on horses who'd thrown shoes before, and I'd never gotten *that* worried.

I glanced at Whisper. "That's what happens when it's *your* horse, huh?"

I stayed with Whisper until the rest of the group was ready to head to The Sweet Shoppe. It had become clear the girls had won when Khloe and Lexa, all smiles, found me and told me to keep my wallet in my bag.

4

BLOGGER
CONFESSIONS

Lauren Towers's Blog
locked post for approved friends only

6:23 p.m.: TGIF, *amis*! (K said I had to translate any French words I wrote because "not everyone's taking French, chica!") She was right! *Amis* means "friends." So . . .

It's finally Friday, and I had a free min to blog! KK and I are heading to C's for a sleepover soon. I've never been in her room, so I'm excited to see how it's decorated and what their tastes are. I could have asked Khloe, but I haven't. It's been more fun to try and guess. But I've been drawing a blank.

Guessing R took control over how the room looks, and the only guess I have is *très* sophisticated and expensive. You know, one of those rooms where you're afraid to touch any-thing because it's worth a gazillion dollars and you don't want to break it. Or a room where everything's white from rugs to bedspreads and you sip soda in the doorway—too afraid to get an orange Slice stain on the rug.

I'm glad it'll be just our little group.

This week has been so crazy! Lessons, classes—busy every second! Sometimes I miss the pace of Yates, and I *always* feel the absence of my friends. It's been hard to keep in touch as much as I wish we could. We're all busy with our own stuff, but I never wanted that to get in the way of our friendships. They're so much more important than sports or debate team. More important than boys, too.

I'm rambling. Sorry! I didn't make this post public because I wanted to use my blog kind of like a journal for a minute.

There's this guy, D, who's on the riding team with me. (I know! I just wrote about friends being more important than guys, but . . .) T and I broke up almost six months ago and I still love him. As a friend.

Now that I've been at CCA a little while, I let my two major rules about Canterwood go out my Hawthorne win-dow: Stay focused on school and work extra hard on riding.

I'm still doing both of those things! But I also said no boys. At least, not until I got used to everything here. I was keeping my promise until I met D. Then I met C.H. (not C.B.) at The SS, and he made me really consider that I could go out with D, but still hold up my end of the bargain about grades and riding.

Besides, Canterwood is so . . . Canterwood. Would I ever know if I was "used" to things here? It changes by the minute, and I don't think that's going away. I have to keep up and have fun. I mean, I'm going to be thirteen (!!) on Halloween, and I don't want to waste any time.

Whoa, LOL. Thirteen sounds sooo cool. I've been wanting to be thirteen forever. I can't go into that—it's an entirely different post! ☺

So I confess, I really, really like D. I could go on and on about his tropical-water blue eyes and dark hair, but ahhh!

No!

K will be out of the shower and ready to go to C's very soon.

The big thing on my mind is my bday. It's, like, six weeks away. I wonder if (a) D will come to my party and (b) if I'll get kissed. ♥

Gotta run!! Just the thought of that will keep me online forever. ☺

Xoxo

Posted by Lauren Towers

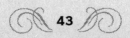

5
RILEY'S ROOM
REVEALED

AN HOUR LATER KHLOE AND I HAD OVERNIGHT
bags packed and headed up to the second floor of Hawthorne
to Clare's room. I'd never climbed the few stairs to the next
level of dorm rooms. The second floor was laid out like the
first, but it felt nice to be a story up. More like my room at
home on the second floor.

"We're going to have *so* much fun," Khloe said. She smiled,
her lips extra shiny from the Laughing Lips Watermelon
Glaze that had come in the mail today from Aerie (our new
fave store). "OMG, if anyone deserves a sleepover—we all
do! The only downer is that Cole can't come."

"I know," I said. "The 'no guys allowed in girls' rooms'
is kind of unfair. If Christina met Cole, she'd see how
sweet he is."

Khloe pouted. "We'll have to work on that. If not for a sleepover, at least getting him over to visit or do homework."

I nodded. Cole was always the perfect icebreaker to any situation. I was a teensy bit nervous about tonight, even though Riley was gone. I guess I wanted to make sure Khloe had fun and forgot where Riley was and what she was doing.

Khloe did a little dance in the hallway. I giggled, snapping out of my thoughts. "It's the best timing *ever* anyway!" she said. "You, Lexa, and I all get to have fun with Clare and not worry that it's going to turn into some kind of Riley's Evil Plot to Ruin the Night."

I grinned. "In my head, I capped the whole 'Evil' part. It felt that important."

Khloe shifted her leather faux-croc bag to the other shoulder. "Um, it *is* that important. No one's going to wake up with their hair chopped off or a can of sticky grape soda poured into their bag."

I shook my head. "Riley's done *those* things during a sleepover?"

Khloe put up both hands, rolling her eyes. "Oh, no one could pin them on Riley. Apparently, Elisa's hair was cut by her secretly jealous roommate, who denied it and started crying. Keep in mind that Elisa's roomie had been intimidated by Riley since day one."

"Suspicious," I said. "And the soda?"

"Riley's hypothesis was that it ended up in *my* bag after being knocked off the table in the middle of the night by accident. Someone did it when they got up to use the bathroom. And it *couldn't* have been Riley, because she's familiar with her own room's layout and wouldn't have run into anything."

I shook my head. "I'd be going back downstairs if Riley were here tonight."

Khloe skipped ahead, flashing a thousand-watt smile, and knocked on Clare's door. "But she's not!"

I looked at Clare and Riley's door. It was so different from the way Khloe and I had decorated ours. The whimsical style hadn't been at all what I'd expected. A chalkboard with pastel chalk was at eye level. Pastel butterfly and flower decals were pressed onto the door. A vinyl banner ran along the top of the door, proudly proclaiming CANTERWOOD CREST ACADEMY EQUESTRIAN TEAM.

"Come in!" Clare's voice was muffled by the door.

I touched the doorknob, noting it had been replaced with a clear crystal knob. Mental note: Ask Clare where she and Riley found it.

"Hey!" I said, opening the door.

"Hi, hi!" Clare said, hurrying over and taking our overnight bags. She put them along the wall and came back, hugging Khloe, then me.

"I'm so glad we're sleeping over!" Khloe said. "Tonight's going to be amaze!"

Clare's blue eyes were extra bright, verging on sapphire. "I know! Lex'll be here any minute."

"Thanks again for inviting me," I said. "I'm so excited. I've been counting down till now."

Clare smiled, genuine and warm. "Of course I'd invite you, Laur. I'm glad you were free."

My eyes surveyed the room. "Wow. It's *gorge* in here."

"Oh!" Clare said. "That's right—you've never been in our room before. Walk around and look at whatever you want."

"Whoa," I said, spotting an extra room. "You and Riley scored a *triple*?"

Clare shrugged, her cheeks getting a little pink. "Riley did that. She arranged it over the summer. I guess we were supposed to have another roommate, but it didn't work out. Christina never moved us, so we got to keep the room."

Khloe snorted. "Was the 'roommate's' name 'Ima Fake?'"

Clare laughed. "Oh, Khloe. Riley would have used a real girl and probably gone as far as getting a birth certificate to score this room."

I surveyed the living-room space. The girls had a small cream-and-lilac love seat facing a massive plasma TV mounted on the wall. Below the TV was a floating bookshelf of DVDs. The ultra-plush cream rug covered most of the shiny hardwood floor, leaving only a little exposed along the wall.

On either side of the love seat were two glass end tables. Each held a lamp with a skinny crystal base that twisted up under a light-pink-and-off-white-striped shade. Pastel coasters with silver stars added pops of color.

"This is beautiful, Clare," I said, gesturing to the love seat and lamps. "Who picked out the stuff?"

Clare smiled. "I did, actually. I asked Riley if I could decorate the entire room this year, since she did it last year. It took, well, a *lot* of convincing before she said yes. I even added the caveat that if she didn't like it, we'd scrap it and she could redo the room."

"Seems like she was happy with it," I said.

"She loves it," Clare said. "I was *desperate* to change up our style from last year—so pristine it felt like I shouldn't sleep in my own bed. Plus, I had a feeling that Riley would love the pastel shades once she saw them in the room."

Khloe looked over at me. "Were you expecting the Princess of Cheer and Light to have black-painted walls or something über-expensive?"

"Maybe not black walls, but I didn't think it would be company friendly."

I walked to the end of the room, where one bed was aligned along the wall. Under the window a nightstand, filled with glittering Swarovski crystal animals, had a reading lamp and iPod dock. In the corner at the opposite side of the room, an ivy plant in a white wicker basket hung down, with tendrils of ivy curling softly.

"That's my bed," Clare said. "Riley's is in the other room, even though technically we can fit two beds in here and one in the smaller room."

"I love it!" I said. Clare's style was girly with a Victorian feel. Her four-poster bed had twinkle lights that wrapped up the posts. The headboard, white painted metal, was an intricate twist. She had piles of light yellow pillows, a matching comforter with splotches of white, and a few stuffed animals: a chestnut horse that looked like Fuego, a hamster with adorable pink ears, and a black-and-white cat with blue eyes. I smiled and picked up a purple My Little Pony.

"I *love* these," I said. "I used to play with them when I was a kid—I don't have any like this, but I want one!"

"Ooh, we should get some!" Khloe said from her spot on the couch. "We should be embarrassed that we, as dedicated equestrians, do not have any My Little Ponies—only the cutest, happiest ponies ever."

Clare grinned and came over to me. "That's Twinkle. I hid her for weeks when I started here last year. I didn't want Riley or anyone to think I was a baby for having stuffed animals. But guess what? Riley has her own."

"Show me!"

I placed Twinkle back among her friends and followed Clare into the "other roommate's" room.

At first I couldn't figure out why Riley would want a smaller room and not just bunk with Clare. There wasn't a door, so it wasn't like she had extra privacy. But then I stepped inside.

"Whoa." It was all I could say.

Khloe and Clare laughed.

"So, what do you think, Laur?" Khloe asked. "You're so quiet."

I was quiet because I felt swallowed by pink and ruffles! R-U-F-F-L-E-S.

"Is this a joke?" I asked, turning to the girls. "Did you

guys do this to Riley's room and hide her real stuff?"

Clare shook her head. "Pinky promise. Never would have guessed it, huh?"

"Never." I inhaled a gentle waft of roses and saw a wall plug-in with a pink cartridge. This could *not* be the lair of Khloe's arch-nemesis, of the girl who'd gone out of her way to make me uncomfortable, or of the girl who I was sure had done awful things that I had yet to learn.

I took another step onto the bubble-gum-pink carpet. Riley had laid four rugs so half the carpet was pink and the other half was white. Her twin bed looked as if it was buried under a foot of bedding—sheets, blankets, comforter. The bedspread, same color as the pink carpet, had tiny white polka dots. The edges of the comforter had layers *and* layers of ruffles.

"How long does it take Riley to move all *those* at night?" I asked, pointing to the pillows on the bed.

There were pink and white pillows of every shape and size imaginable. I recognized a few round ones with ruffles that spiraled into the center from Pottery Barn Teen.

"She's got it down to a science," Clare said. "Not as long as you'd think."

There was a knock on the door, and Clare excused herself to answer it. I heard Lexa's voice and then Clare's say, "Lauren just discovered the Room of Pink."

"Ooh," Lexa said, laughing. She stepped into Riley's room with Clare and stood near Khloe and me. "Hey!"

"Hi!" Khloe and I said simultaneously.

"I forgot that this was your first time here," Lexa said. "Did you ever think for a nanosecond that Riley Edwards's room would look like this?"

I shook my head. "Even the curtains are pink!" The windows were decked out in sheer pink curtains, with a heavier velvet pink curtain over the top. They were held back by white ties. *Ruffled* white ties.

"I mean, I have a favorite color and it does dominate my room," I said, still glancing around from one pink object to the next. "There's nothing wrong with decorating your room however you like, but I did *not* expect this from Riley."

Khloe touched a silver photo frame adorned with pink crystals. "I thought about telling you first, but you seeing it like this was oh-so-delicious."

I walked over to Riley's desk, which had two white bookcases on either side. There were a few books, mostly equine-related, held by wooden heart bookends.

The rest of the space was filled with framed photos. Photos that didn't reflect the Riley I knew. One was a gorge close-up of Adonis, his gaze soft as he looked into the camera. A setting sun cast a gentle light on his neck. Another shot was of Clare and Riley, sitting bareback on Fuego and Adonis. No bridles, just their fingers intertwined in manes. Lush trees made a vibrant green background, and both girls were in T-shirts and shorts. I'd never seen Riley look like that . . . blissful.

"C'mon, guys," Clare said. "Let's forget about Riley for a night and get our party started."

6

LIST-MAKER
CLARE

"LET'S DO IT!" LEXA SAID. WE FOLLOWED
Clare out of Riley's room and settled around the living
room table.

There was a sheet of notebook paper in the center, and
"Sleepover Stuff!!" was written in super-neat, tiny hand-
writing across the top. Clare started to move the paper
toward her, but Khloe put her hand on top of Clare's.

"What's this?" Khloe asked.

Clare's face turned red, making her freckles invis-
ible. "Just a silly list that I made. Of stuff. Stuff to do.
Sleepover stuff."

"Wow, you made actual plans?" Lexa asked, pulling her
curly hair into a messy ponytail. She made a worried face.
"Maybe I should do that. I don't want mine to be boring!"

Clare shook her head, a red curl loosening from her clip. "No, no. It's not like that. It's . . . well, I've never had my own sleepover before. Riley is always the hostess. She decides everything we do. And don't do. And eat. And watch on TV. We always have fun, and I didn't even think until a few hours ago that this was *my* sleepover."

"I bet I can speak for all of us when I say I *know* we're going to have fun," I said. "I'm so excited to be here."

"Me too," Khloe said, patting her friend's hand. "I'm sorry if you got stressed or thought we wouldn't have fun. Want us to look at your list and see what you've got?"

Clare nodded. "Maybe. Okay. Yes."

I tried not to make the face I knew that I wouldn't want—the oh-poor-you face. Instead I looked at the list with the other girls.

SLEEPOVER STUFF!!

Movies (?) but will anyone want to watch one? Who picks? What if I only have boring ones?

Snacks. Make sure to get something *everybody* likes!!

TV series on DVD. Same prob as movies.

Board games. (Are those lame?)

Nails?

Prank call boys?

I stopped before I read the rest and looked up from the paper. "Clare," I said, "this is a great list!"

Clare glanced up from her nails, where she'd been picking at the polish. "Really?"

"Really!" Lexa, Khloe, and I said at the same time. It made us all giggle.

"You don't need Riley or anyone else to plan a sleepover, Clare," Lexa said. "I *totally* get being nervous to host one, but you've been to enough to know what to do. Plus, you know us. I'm definitely chill doing whatever."

"Me too," Khloe said. She shot Lexa a quick smile. Clare and Lexa weren't BFFs, because of Clare's friendship with Riley. But Lexa had just been the first one to assure Clare of her sleepover capabilities. I knew it made Khloe feel good to see two of her besties getting along.

"We can do *all* the things on your list, none of them, or some," I said. "It's your room, and you can decide what we do or we can all decide together."

Clare smiled. "Thanks, guys. You're making me feel so much better about this. I'd love for all of us to pick."

We all nodded in agreement.

"Nails, anyone?" Khloe asked. "Mine are *gross*, and they have, like, polish on every other finger."

"I sooo need mine done!" Lexa raised her hand as if

she was waiting for a teacher to call on her.

In minutes Clare had pulled out a *giant* plastic bin of polish.

"Whoa," Lexa said, peering inside. "That's a lot of—"

She stopped when Clare put down a second bin, popped off the top, and grinned. "In case there weren't enough colors to choose from . . . these are Riley's."

Between the two girls, every brand and color was available.

"Love how you mix expensive polishes with drugstore brands," I said. "Just because the bottle says 'Chanel' doesn't automatically make it a good polish."

"Agreed!" Clare said, sitting cross-legged next to me. "I love Wet n Wild, Sally Hansen—all those you can buy at the drugstore."

Each of us picked up different bottles, and no one had the same color choice. I finally settled on a matte-gray OPI, Khloe picked a taxicab-yellow Revlon, Clare fell in love with an emerald-green Essie, and Lexa chose a shimmery caramel Deborah Lippman.

"I know the rest of you guys know this," I said, turning to Clare. "But what's your background? Where are you from? I don't know much about you."

Clare rubbed a polish-remover-soaked cotton ball over

her thumb, smiling. "These guys *do* know, so I'll try to make it interesting. I was born in Texas but moved to a tiny town just about twenty minutes away from here when I was two. So Connecticut's my home."

"Can totally picture you growing up in Texas," Khloe said, sticking out her tongue. "Tumbleweeds, armadillos, giant snakes . . ."

Clare gave her friend a mock evil eye. "If I had grown up there, you left out one thing: cute cowboys."

Lexa, Khloe, and I laughed.

"Touché," Khloe said.

"So, you escaped the tumbleweeds, armadillos, monster snakes, and cute cowboys practically before you could talk," I said. "What's your family like?"

"So normal that it's seriously boring," Clare said. "My dad's a dentist, Mom works at the local bank, and I've got a chocolate Lab that I've considered petitioning to bring to school with me."

"We really could use a dorm hall mascot," Lexa said, smiling. "I love dogs. I had a cocker spaniel when I lived in London."

"Yeaaah," I said. "About that. What's the deal with London? What do your parents do?"

Lexa looked up from painting her index finger. "I lived

there for a year when I was ten. Didn't pick up the accent or anything."

"Tragic," Khloe murmured.

Lexa shook her head. "Lucky for me, Khlo, no one has ever asked me to read with a British accent."

"I meant tragic for *moi*," Khloe said. "I want to learn accents, and you could have coached me."

We all laughed. So Khloe was obsessed with her acting. Her determination to "make it" was inspiring, to me, anyway.

"We'll rent a bunch of Brit flicks and they'll help you," I said.

The other girls nodded.

"Sorry," Khloe said, shaking her head. "Lex, I totally derailed your London convo."

"No, you didn't. All I really had left to say was that I wish I could have lived there longer. I was too young to really appreciate everything about the city."

"Why just a year?" Clare asked.

"Witness protection," Lexa said. "Mom's background as an ex-spy comes with some strings."

My mouth fell open. I snapped it shut, feeling like a huge dork. "S-spy?" I asked.

Lexa looked over, holding my gaze. "Top secret. It can't leave this room."

I just stared at her, then nodded. I sneaked a glance at Clare, whose eyes were wide like a spooked horse.

Lexa grinned. "Sorry, Clare and LT. I always play the spy card on new people. Like Clare thinks her family is boring, mine is too. I only lived in London because my mom was transferred to her company's European branch."

I gave her an exaggerated sigh. "You and Khloe are perfect for each other. Khloe pretended to hate me the second we met, and you made me think I'd befriended a girl with a spy for a parent."

We tossed around stories of what we'd thought when we first met each other. The conversation was easy, and soon our nails were drying.

Khloe picked up her phone and opened an app. I recognized Chatter. Lexa and Clare, deep in conversation about the upcoming schooling show, didn't notice. Khloe scrolled through updates and, stopping on one, frowned.

I could only guess whose update she had read.

"Sounds like Riley's doing awesome in New York," Khloe said. Her usually upbeat tone was flat.

Clare and Lexa looked up.

"Why do you think that?" Lexa asked.

"Because of Chatter. I haven't let myself check Riley's updates for two whole days, and I finally did. She's

Chatting update after update about how she's killing her audition and how much she loves New York City."

Khloe held her BlackBerry up to us. There was a photo of a grinning Riley, standing at night in Times Square. Billboards glowed and glittered all around her.

"Don't let *Riley* ruin this," I said. "Like Clare said, we never get a chance to sleep over here."

"Plus, you know Riley's a li—" Lexa stopped, looking at Clare. "I mean, you know Riley exaggerates. Maybe she is doing great. But I bet a lot of other actors are too."

Clare inspected her nails, looking as if she was measuring her words, then looked at Khloe. "Riley hasn't told me much about what's going on. But whatever happens, I don't want to waste tonight thinking about something we have zero control over."

Khloe took a long breath and shoved her phone across the room. "You're right. Sorry, guys. There's so much awesome stuff to talk about." A giant smile spread across her face, and she looked at me. "Like, something to do with our very own Lauren Towers."

I looked at her sideways. "Me?"

"Yes, you." She looked at the other girls. "I met Laur's sister, Rebecca, on Skype, and *she* told me something that LT had neglected to mention. Something vital."

Clare and Lexa's attention was no longer on their nails. They watched Khloe, waiting for the rest.

"Lauren's birthday is coming up!" Khloe said. She flashed me a smile. "It's only on one of the coolest days of the year—Halloween!"

"Lauren!" Lexa and Clare said at the same time.

"How come you didn't tell us?" Lexa asked.

"Yeah!" Clare said. "We obvi need time to plan you a killer first Canterwood birthday party."

I waved a hand. "I was going to bring it up. There was a lot going on when Becca told Khlo."

Clare sipped her orange soda. "Not much is more important than your *thirteenth* birthday that happens to fall on Halloween. There are *so* many things we can do with this. Ahhh! I'm excited."

Lexa put away her nail polish. "Me too! We're going to throw you a birthday bash like Canterwood's never seen. Ooh, I can't wait."

I smiled. It felt amazing to have my friends so excited about my birthday. They were all looking forward to it, and I was glad that Khloe had brought it up.

"Promise me one thing?" I asked.

"Anything," Khloe said.

"There's plenty of time *after* the schooling show to

plan. So, if you *were* going to start thinking up ideas, will you wait until after we compete? I want all your free time to go to practicing."

The three girls looked at one another.

"Deal," they said in unison.

7
SLEEPOVER INTERRUPTED!

THE REST OF THE NIGHT WAS SPENT IN TRUE sleepover fashion. We had pizza delivered, watched a couple of movies, and put face masks on each other. Clare had just gotten a new pineapple enzyme mask that we all wanted to try.

"We smell like the beach," I said, laughing. The clear goop on my face made my skin tingle.

"I'll happily take smelling like a picnic basket if it means tiny pores," Lexa said.

"Ditto," Khloe said.

My phone chimed, and I reached over to grab it off Clare's bed. It was late, and all my friends were here—who was BBMing me?

I opened BBM and saw *Drew* lit up.

Drew:

How's ur nite?

I typed back.

Lauren:

Great! @ Clare's 4 a sleepover.

Drew:

U watching chick flicks & talking abt guys?

Lauren:

LOL. Maybe.

Drew:

I'll let u go. U guys wanna trail ride w me 2mrw?

Lauren:

Lemme ask & I'll let u know!

I tossed my phone down and turned around. Khloe, Clare, and Lexa were staring at me with expectant looks on their faces.

"What?" I asked, giggling.

"Oh, this will take *so* much longer if you play the innocent act," Khloe said. "What's Drew up to?"

Anytime his name was mentioned, I couldn't help but blush. It was the most annoying reaction, but I couldn't stop it. Maybe the pineapple mask concealed some of it. . . .

"He was seeing what I was doing," I said.

"Aw!" the girls said simultaneously.

"It was *so* not a big deal," I said. "But he did ask if we wanted to trail ride with him tomorrow."

"First, it *was* a big deal," Khloe said. "He messaged you on Friday night! He could have been playing Xbox or doing whatever boys do, and he stopped to say 'hi' to you. He was thinking about you."

"So romantic," Clare said with a happy sigh. "Drew Adams like-likes our LT."

I tried not to give too much weight to Clare's words, but I wanted them to be true. I knew that Drew liked me and I liked him. A lot. But I didn't want to jump into anything too fast.

"What about the second part?" I asked, pulling my pjs out of my bag. "You guys up for a trail ride tomorrow?"

"YES!"

Everyone's near shout almost knocked me off my toes, where I was digging through my overnight bag.

"I think I have your answers," I said, grinning. "And we're going to be lucky if the entire floor didn't hear that."

We all changed into our pajamas, and I crawled into my sleeping bag.

"I'll write Drew tomorrow morning and say that we're up for it," I said. "Whisper's getting shod in the morning, and then she'll be all set."

"I'm going to be at the stable most of the day tomorrow," Clare said. She pulled back the covers on her bed. "So I'm game for whenever."

Easy, quiet talk continued until each girl fell asleep. I was the last one awake, and I pulled my sleeping bag top over my head as I turned on my phone. I didn't want the backlight to wake anyone.

I read through my conversation with Drew. Smiling, I typed a message.

Lauren:

I hope ur phone's off & this doesn't wake u if ur asleep. Wanted 2 say we'd all love 2 trail ride 2mrw. Whenever ur free, let me know. C u then.

I sent the message and opened Chatter. I read a few updates from my friends.

AnaArtiste: No hmwk this wkend! Get 2 work with new oil paints. ☺

There was a short convo between Brielle and Taylor.

BrielleisaBeauty: @TFrost: The movie was amaze!

TFrost: @BrielleisaBeauty: Way better than I thought it would b.

BrielleisaBeauty: @TFrost: Totally. C u tmrw.

I read the message again. The message didn't say whether any of our other friends from Yates had gone, too. It sounded as if it had been just Brielle and Taylor.

But did I care? *Should* I care? I was kind of seeing someone else, and Taylor and I weren't together anymore.

Then I saw another message.

AnaArtiste: @BrielleisaBeauty @TFrost: Loved the movie!!

I wanted to smack myself. Ana had been there too. I had to stop jumping to conclusions. Besides, *I* had written one-on-one exchanges with Drew and hadn't thought about Taylor seeing them and reading into it.

I clicked on my profile and typed a new status update.

LaurBell: Sleepover @CutieClare's w @DramaRama & @Lexaaa was so fun. Every1's asleep now. Night! Zzzz...

I updated my status, poked my head out of my sleeping bag, and fell asleep with my phone in hand.

8

A CHATTER
ADDICTION CAN
RUIN A SLEEPOVER

"LAAAUREEEN."

I opened my eyes, blinking at the unfamiliar surroundings. Then I remembered I was at Clare's.

Khloe was crouched beside me, her blond hair wavy and her braid messy from sleep.

"What?" I asked. Everyone else was still sleeping, and gentle sunlight filtered through Clare's shades.

Khloe looked over her shoulder at Lexa, who turned over in her sleeping bag, breathing deeply. Then she looked up at Clare, who had a purple mask over her eyes.

"Come on," Khloe whispered.

I started to ask, but the look on Khloe's face stopped me. Something was wrong. Khloe was *never* the first one awake, and she looked like she'd been up for a while. There weren't any signs of sleepiness on her face—instead her mouth was pressed together, and she was clenching and unclenching her fingers.

Without a word, I crawled out of my warm sleeping bag, then grabbed slippers and my blue robe to throw over my white shorts and lace eyelet tank top.

Khloe eased open the door, made sure it was unlocked, and motioned me to go in front of her. We stepped into the silent hallway, and I slid into my slippers and pulled on my robe.

"Okay. You're scaring me. What's going on?" I asked her.

Khloe rubbed her forehead. "We've got a Riley problem."

We walked a few steps away from Clare's door, and Khloe plopped onto the floor, patting the carpet next to her.

I was still sleepy. "What do you mean? Riley's not even here."

Khloe held out her phone and handed me mine. "I grabbed yours," she explained. "You updated your Chatter status last night."

"Yeah . . . ," I said, dragging out the word. "So? I don't understand."

"You wrote that we were staying at Clare's." Khloe

rubbed her forehead. "It's so dumb that it's an issue, but Clare didn't tell Riley that Lexa, you, and I were sleeping over. Riley would have said no way and been really ticked at Clare for asking."

Suddenly, I got it. "And you said Clare didn't even talk to Riley about it. So she probably wasn't going to even tell Riley that we slept over," I said, drawing my knees up to my chest.

Khloe picked at the fresh polish on her thumb. "She definitely wasn't going to say a word. Clare's going to get ripped from Riley for having us over."

"Oh, no. Oh, Khlo. I didn't even think last night. I should have. But wait, it's early in the morning. I posted that *really* late last night. What if Riley didn't even see it? I can delete it right now and Riley will never know."

Khloe gave me a small smile. "If only Riley wasn't a Chatter addict who checks it every two seconds. She already saw it. Check your phone."

I turned on my BlackBerry and there were Chatter notifications. I went straight to the replies.

OfficiallyRiley: Wow! Seems like my bestie, @CutieClare, doesn't miss me at all. She already filled our room w new roomies—@Lexaaa, @DramaRama, & @LaurBell.

That was posted hours after I'd written my message.

There were individual messages from Riley to each of us, all written minutes apart this morning.

OfficiallyRiley: @CutieClare: I'm coming back tmrw, Clare. Hope that doesn't disappoint u 2 much.

"Are you kidding me?" I asked. "This is so immature!" I felt sick that I'd caused trouble between Clare and Riley. Poor, sleeping Clare had no idea yet about what she was going to wake up to. All because I'd been missing half my brain last night.

Khloe shook her head. "I wish this was a joke. Keep reading."

OfficiallyRiley: @Lexaaa: Did u have fun sleeping in my dorm room, Lex? R @CutieClare & I invited 2 ur room next? We'd def want Jill's OK first, tho.

The girl was transparent. She was broadcasting what read like some kind of ultimate betrayal on Chatter and painting Clare like a girl who couldn't wait to get rid of her roommate to have people over.

OfficiallyRiley: @DramaRama: *claps* Bravo, KK! Good move sleeping over while I was away. 2 bad u just got 2 sleep on my floor while I slept in NYC.

I couldn't look at Khloe when I read that message. I knew how competitive the two girls were with acting. Khloe had to be practically burning from that.

OfficiallyRiley: @LaurBell: So glad u had a bonding nite, new girl! If u moved any of my riding trophies, could u make sure they're back in place? PS: Are u having urs sent here now that the word's out, dressage champ?

I exited the application and squeezed my eyes shut. "Great. What now? It's my fault, so I'm obviously telling Clare. What if I BMM Riley an apology and say Clare told us we couldn't sleep over, but we kept bugging her until she said yes?"

Khloe shook her head. "Riley's smarter than that. I think all we can do is tell Clare and let her decide how to handle it. She's my best friend, but she's Riley's, too. At first I wanted to do something immediately to fix it for Clare, but I can't. She has to decide if she's going to start standing up for herself against Riley."

"I'm sorry, Khloe," I said quietly. "I know this isn't an easy situation for you. I can't imagine how hard it is to have Clare be so tight with someone who treats you like trash."

"I've kind of learned to live with it," Khloe said. She leaned her head against the wall. "Clare and Riley were friends first. Then I met Clare, and we became friends on our own. When Clare introduced me to Riley, she was really hoping the three of us would all get along. It just didn't work out that way. At all."

"It's made things difficult for you and Lexa, too," I said. "But I want you to know how much I like Clare and that I support your friendship with her. From how Lexa acted last night, I think she and Clare have a shot at becoming friends."

Khloe nodded. "Lexa and Clare got along really well. Face it—everyone gets along better without Riley around." She closed her eyes for a second. "I almost wish that Riley would get the acting gig in New York."

"She won't," I said firmly. "It would be easier without Riley here, but she's not going to get the job, Khlo. We'll have to learn how to coexist. Somehow."

Khloe patted my arm. "You're a good friend, LT. I guess we should go back before anyone wakes up and worries that we're gone."

"Agreed," I said, standing and offering a hand to Khloe. "And I'm going to tell Clare right away. I don't want Riley to have a chance to say anything else over Chatter."

We padded the few steps back to Clare and Riley's, and I opened the door. Khloe shut the door behind us and I kicked off my slippers, taking a breath. I hoped Clare wouldn't hate me because of what I'd done.

It had gotten much lighter outside, and the clock beside Clare changed to 9:02 a.m. I leaned down to put my phone on my pillow, and Lexa shifted in her sleeping bag, blinking and looking up at me.

"Hey," she whispered.

"Morning," I said.

Lexa rolled onto her stomach, propping herself up on her elbows. Her eyes shifted to Khloe, who'd sat on the edge of the coffee table. The friends waved at each other.

Sheets rustled and Clare reached up to her face, pulling off her eye mask. A few red curls stuck up, having escaped from their ponytail. She yawned and smiled sleepily at us.

"You guys been up long?" she asked, sitting up.

Lexa shook her head. "Not even a minute."

Clare looked at the clock. "Did we fail sleepover morning after by not sleeping until noon?"

We laughed, but mine was forced, and I had a feeling Khloe's was as well.

"Nah," Khloe said. "Who wants to waste weekend minutes? We've all got stuff at the stable to do, and I'm excited about trail riding."

"Me too," I said.

Clare looked at her nightstand again. "Geez, my phone's blinking like crazy." She started to reach for it.

"Clare," I said. "Wait a sec. I need to tell you something."

Slowly, Clare pulled back her hand. "Okaaay." She looked at Khloe. "Something happened. What?"

That made Lexa sit up.

I sat next to Khloe on the coffee table, facing Clare.

"I messed up last night," I said. "I was awake after you guys fell asleep. I wrote Drew back that we all wanted to trail ride with him."

Clare shook her head. "Not seeing how you messed up."

"Then I got on Chatter." I took a big breath. *Please don't let Clare freak out,* I thought. "I wrote about what an awesome time I was having last night. Sleeping over *here* with you, Khloe, and Lex."

Clare sat up straighter. "You said you guys were sleeping here?" She played with the strap on her eye mask. "I didn't tell Riley."

"I know," I said. "Clare, I'm so, so sorry. This morning, Khloe saw what I'd done and we were going to erase my message, but it's too late. Riley saw it already, and she sent nasty messages to each of us. It's all my fault. I promise that I'll do anything you want to smooth things over between you and Riley."

Clare shook her head and reached for her phone. I watched as she stared at the screen for what felt like forever. She typed something, then put down the phone.

Then she looked back at me, her expression blank. It was official: Clare was mad at me. I couldn't blame her. I never should have sent the message.

"Clare," Khloe said, "we're going to help with Riley. I know you're upset, but please try to remember that this is *your* room too. You don't need anyone's permission to have friends over."

Clare nodded. "I know. I BBMed Riley and told her that I'd wanted you all to stay over. I told her I would have asked if she'd been here, but she wasn't." She looked at me. "Please don't feel like you did something wrong. You didn't. I'm sorry that all you guys got messages from Riley."

"Wait, wait," Lexa said. "You're serious? You basically told Riley to get over it? No offense, but I thought you'd be freaking out. You kind of . . ."

Lexa let her sentence go without finishing.

Clare pulled back her covers and walked to the floor, then sat down by all of us. She smoothed her oversize red I ♥ BOYS T-shirt, which she'd paired with black leggings. "I kind of always bow down to Riley. Or do whatever she says. It's okay, Lexa. I know that."

"What made you write her something like that *now*?" Khloe asked. "Clare, she's one of your best friends."

"Exactly. And a 'best friend' shouldn't act like that.

It's one thing if Riley wants to freak out at me, but I'm not letting her do that to all of you." Clare looked down. "And Khloe, I'm so sorry. I let Riley get away with a lot of things that she's said and done to you. I'm your best friend, and you deserve to have me act like one. I'm going to start doing a better job."

Khloe's eyes got misty. She got up and leaned down to hug Clare. "Thanks, C. But I want you to keep your friendship with Riley, if you want."

They let go of each other, and Clare nodded. "I will. But some things have to change. She's Riley Edwards. I don't expect her to suddenly be sugary sweet to everyone, but the insults have to stop."

Lexa reached out an arm and hugged Clare. "You're brave. It's not easy to do what you did."

Clare shook her head. "I should have done that a long time ago."

I hugged Clare too. "Again, I'm sorry things happened this way. Remember that we're all here for you, and maybe we can get Riley on board with the idea that it's easier to be civil than to talk nasty about each other."

Clare squeezed me. "We'll see, huh?"

The four of us looked at each other. Khloe was the first to smile, and soon the rest of us did too.

"Maybe Riley and I will be friends by my birthday party and she'll give me a treat and not a trick!" I said.

We giggled.

"I think that's a good goal, Laur," Lexa said.

Clare got off the floor, stretching, and started to make her bed. "Breakfast, change clothes, then head to stable?" she asked.

"Done," I said.

Khloe and Lexa added their yeses. By the time we walked to the common room, it felt as though a piece of Clare had disappeared. It had been replaced by confidence that was trying to break through the surface of the girl who'd always followed at Riley's heels.

"Oh, check your Chatter, everyone," Clare said as we walked into the common room.

We pulled out our phones. I smiled as I read the update.

CutieClare: Ready 4 trail ride w @DramaRama, @Lexaaa, @LaurBell, & @SwmerGuy. Xcited 4 @OfficiallyRiley 2 b back tmrw!

SHOE SHOPPING
OF A DIFFERENT
KIND

I SNAPPED A LEAD LINE TO WHISPER'S HAL-
ter and kissed her cheek.

"Ready for new shoes?" I asked. "They'll be all shiny
and pretty."

Whisper made wide eyes at me. She wasn't a huge fan
of being shod, but she always seemed to prance in her new
horseshoes when the process was over. Since she needed
new shoes every six to eight weeks, I was glad Whisper
seemed happy in the end. We were next for the farrier. I'd
made it to the stable in time to groom Whisper before
her turn.

After a breakfast of Lucky Charms and tea, the girls
and I had gone back to Clare's room and cleaned up our
stuff. We'd changed, and I'd told everyone I'd let them

know when Whisper was finished and ready to be tacked up for our trail ride.

I'd found a message from Drew when I'd checked my phone after breakfast.

Drew:

Glad u guys want 2 trail ride. If u don't c me, msg me when Whisper's ready & we can meet out front 20 mins afr that.

I led Whisper out of her box stall to the front of the stable where Mr. Farley, the farrier, had his tools set up. He and Mr. Conner were talking.

"Ah, Lauren," Mr. Conner said. "Brent, this is Lauren and her mare, Whisper. They're new to Canterwood."

"Nice to meet you," Mr. Farley said, rubbing his hands on his leather apron. "You'll be seeing a lot of me." He smiled, showing tan lines on his face. I had a good feeling about him, which was critical whenever I let anyone work on Whisper. Mr. Farley had kind brown eyes that matched his buzzed hair.

"It's good to meet you, too," I replied.

"We want to make sure, Brent, that the hoof with a missing shoe isn't tender," Mr. Conner said.

"Let's get the mare into cross-ties and I'll take a look," Mr. Farley said, brushing a hand over his brow. He'd probably been shoeing horses all morning. His forearms were

streaked with dirt, and he had a trash can full of hoof clip-
pings off to the side.

I cross-tied Whisper and stood near her head, keeping
one hand on her halter.

Mr. Farley walked over to the hoof in question, murmur-
ing soothing words to Whisper.

I'd seen a few bad farriers on the show circuit—some
who were impatient when horses acted up and others who
lacked proper training. Even though Mr. Farley seemed
nice, I was *très* protective of *mon amour* (my love!), and I
was going to watch every second—as much as I trusted
Mr. Conner to have a top farrier on call.

Mr. Farley picked up her hoof and cradled it between
his knees. He reached into his apron pocket and pulled out
a pair of tongs. I tried to cross my toes, since my hands
were busy. I peered to the side and saw Mr. Farley run his
thumb over her hoof, pressing on the frog, or V-shaped
part. Whisper didn't react to his touch. Nor did she move
when he applied more pressure with the metal tongs.

"Looks fine to me," Mr. Farley said. "I don't see any
hint of soreness."

"Yay," I said quietly, stroking Whisper's cheek. In my
gut, I hadn't thought she was sore, but I knew I'd never
feel at ease until Wisp got a once-over from a professional.

Mr. Farley kept her hind leg in his grasp and trimmed her hoof with a pair of nippers. Whisper didn't mind this part. After trimming, he used a hoof knife to slice and trim around the frog and sole of her hoof. Then he picked a shoe out of his apron, eyeing the fit. He released Whisper's hoof, moved to the portable forge, and stuck the shoe inside. Soon the metal shoe was red-hot. Mr. Farley used his anvil and a hammer to shape the shoe, then dunked it into a bucket of cold water, making the metal sizzle. Many farriers I'd watched would place the hot shoe on the horse's hoof for a few seconds to see if the fit was right, but I liked that Mr. Farley was doing a mix of hot and cold shoeing.

Whisper's ears had gone back when the hammering started, and she swished her tail when the horseshoe sizzled.

"It's okay," I said. "None of this hurts, remember?"

Mr. Conner stood, silent, watching the process. I wondered if he was sticking by in case I needed help with Whisper.

Mr. Farley lifted her back hoof again and placed the shoe on the bare hoof.

"Perfect fit," he said. "I'm going to hammer it into place now."

"Okay," I said. I grasped Whisper's halter a little tighter. "We're going on a trail ride after this." I raised my voice so she could hear me above the hammering. "It's going to be really fun, *and* it'll be practice for the show. Sound like a plan?"

I kept talking and was deep in conversation with Whisper about my newest beauty find from Sephora when I looked up. Mr. Farley and Mr. Conner were standing together by the forge, smiling at me.

"Lauren, what was the name of that nail polish you were about to share with Whisper?" Mr. Conner asked. He laughed kindly, and Mr. Farley joined in.

"You're finished?" I asked.

Mr. Farley nodded. "She's good to go. She was so well behaved, Lauren. I look forward to shoeing her again."

Pride made me smile. "Thank you, sir. I appreciate your time and being gentle with her."

I unclipped Whisper from the cross-ties and led her back to her stall. Then I took out my phone and BBMed Drew, Khloe, Clare, and Lexa.

Lauren:

Whisper has new shoes & I'm gonna tack up. Meet u outside soon?

While I gathered Whisper's tack, I got messaged back from everyone that they'd be ready soon.

Since Whisper was already groomed, I tied her to the inside of her stall and picked up the bubble-gum-pink saddle pad that I saved for fun occasions. It took minutes to get her saddled and bridled.

Whisper lifted her hooves high as we went down the aisle to the main entrance. I was glad she'd have time to get used to the new shoes before the show.

"Knew it!" I said. "You heart your shoes."

We exited the stable and stopped at the side of the double doors. It was the perfect day to trail ride. The late September air had the slightest hint of coolness. The stickiness of summer was gone, but the midmorning sun blazed in the sky. A few thin, wispy clouds lingered in the sky, allowing most of the brilliant blue sky to be as visible as possible.

I put on my helmet and mounted. I'd just raked my fingers though my wavy hair when a horse and rider emerged from the stable.

"Hi," Drew said, looking up at me. "Ready to ride?"

10

PLAYING GAMES

"HEY," I SAID. I LOOKED INTO HIS BLUE eyes—bluer than almost anything I'd ever seen. I got goose bumps and was glad I'd thrown on a light gray jacket.

Whisper reached her muzzle toward Polo. The gelding stretched his muzzle back, and they huffed at each other. Whisper blinked, batting her long eyelashes and turning her head slightly to the side.

My horse was a better flirt than I was!

Drew mounted, swinging a leg over Polo's back and settling into the saddle. He looked *parfait*. His ease with Polo made it hard to look away, not to mention the T-shirt that matched his eyes, black zip-up jacket, and tan breeches.

"I'm glad you were free today," Drew said. "I needed

to get out of the stable. Trail riding is like running—it's a stress buster."

"Same for me," I said. "I'm glad you asked me and my friends. We kind of need a break too. Stressful week."

Drew made a face. "Sorry. But this will make you forget about it."

"Hellooo!" Lexa said, leading Honor. She was flanked by Clare with Fuego and Khloe with Ever.

All three of them shifted their eyes between Drew and me. I shot them a *say-anything-and-die* look, and when Drew's eyes weren't on me, I made a slashing motion across my throat.

Khloe started to laugh but covered it with a cough.

"Thanks for inviting us," Clare said.

"Yeah," Khloe added, mounting Ever. "I would have a mental breakdown if I had to do one more spiral in the arena right now."

"Mental breakdown, huh?" Drew said, looking mock serious. "We better get on the trail fast."

"Def," Lexa said. "Khlo, you know I love you, but you're already *this close* to crazy. I don't want to see what happens if Khloe Kinsella is pushed over the edge."

We all laughed.

"Let's go!" I said.

87

The four of us turned our horses away from the stable yard and headed for the woods on the outer edge of the campus.

I somehow (ahem, thanks, Khloe) ended up next to Drew, with Lexa to my right and Clare beside her. Whisper's body language changed the second she realized we weren't going into the arena. I felt her muscles loosen, a swing fell into her stride, and she shook her head, sending her mane scattering.

I laughed. "Someone's happy not to be practicing."

"I'd shake my mane too," Khloe said, grinning. "This feels so good!"

The four of us let our horses trot, and we posted as we left the stable behind and headed for the trees and the woodland area. The campus, beautiful from every angle, looked especially *très belle* from here. We were headed down a gentle slope, and all that was visible of the campus were tops of buildings and streetlamps.

"I'm so glad to leave everything behind," I said.

"Me too," Drew said.

"The campus is like its own city," Clare said. "Know what I mean? Our entire lives are contained in this one spot where we do everything."

Everyone nodded at that.

"We can't escape the people we're with. *Ever.* We may have separate dorm halls or rooms from people we see in class or whatever, but it's like living in a small town. It feels like there's always the possibility of running into someone."

"I get that," I said, easing Whisper to a walk as we approached the line of trees that flanked a dirt trail. "It's like everyone knows *everything* that's going on with each other. Like sometimes we're all a bunch of gossipy older women I've seen at salons, sitting under dryers with their wet curls."

"Um, I have never, nor will I ever, sit under a dryer and gossip," Drew said. He raised both eyebrows, shooting me a glance. A smile tugged at the corner of his mouth. It made my palms a little sweaty against the reins.

Clare, Lex, and I giggled at his pretend offense.

"We're not including you in our gossipy olds count," Khloe said.

Drew put a hand over his heart, neck-reining Polo. "Whew. So relieved you don't see me that way."

Clare and Fuego and Khloe and Ever entered the trail first with Lexa close behind, followed by Drew and me.

"Up for a new trail, LT?" Khloe asked.

"*Oui!*" I said. "Always."

"Guys, is the one following the creek to the meadow okay?" Khloe asked.

"Perf," Clare said.

Drew added a yes, and we kept walking through the woods. We walked the horses under a canopy of trees, and I took a mental snapshot of the scenery. The light filtered through the trees, casting shadows of all shapes and sizes onto the dirt trail.

"It's so gorgeous," I said to Drew. "Look at the way the sunlight reflects on those leaves."

I tilted my head toward some maple leaves, and Drew followed my gaze.

"I like how you notice those things," he said. "You've got this attention to details that no one else sees."

I blushed. "I'm definitely not the only one—"

Drew shook his head, stopping me. "Try to let me finish my compliment. You're way too humble to say anything, but I want to."

I looked at Whisper's mane, then back up at him. "Okay, okay. Go."

Drew smiled, satisfied. "I didn't even look at the leaves, but once you pointed them out, I took a closer look. You notice the beautiful things, Lauren, that I think most people walk right by."

His words silenced me. I forgot where I was, what we were doing, and who I was talking to for a second. Then I snapped back to reality, staring at him. "Wow. No one has ever said anything like that to me before. Thanks, Drew. That was so sweet."

"Just calling it like I see it," he said.

I grinned and looked ahead, seeing that Lexa had slowed Honor so she was closer to us. I was so calling her on that later. Eavesdropper! But I wasn't mad.

"Right at the next fork," Khloe called.

We made the turn, and the dirt trail widened so we could ride side by side.

The woods were peaceful, and I couldn't imagine anything else I'd rather be doing.

"Want to play games while we ride?" Drew asked. He was still next to me, with Clare on his right, then Khloe. Lexa had ended up to my left.

"Totally!" Clare said.

"I *miss* games!" Lexa said. "Remember when those actually counted as a lesson?"

"If only we could convince Mr. Conner that passing the flag or an egg-and-spoon challenge was a good lesson," I said, giggling.

Khloe frowned. "I always dropped the eggs. Once, when I was in Pony Club and competing against another chapter, I lost so many eggs that they ran *out*! How does *that* happen? One of my most embarrassing moments ever in the horse world!"

"We're so doing that one day," Clare said. "We'll get a bunch of riders together and play. Khlo, maybe we'll glue your egg to your spoon or something."

Khloe nodded, patting Ever's neck. "Done. I'm so not above that."

We approached the fork in the trail and veered to the right. The path was free of debris, minus a few branches, and it was wider than the path we'd been on.

"Okay," Drew said. "Everybody stand in your stirrups. No holding onto manes or anything. You sit, you're out."

I felt my competitive juices kick in. We all stood and I glanced at Drew, a cool, *this-is-so-easy* look on my face.

"Guys! Look at the deer!" Khloe said.

I swiveled my head and immediately lost my balance. Not wanting to pull on Whisper's mouth, I sat down.

Everyone else was standing.

Shoot. Going out the first round wasn't fun.

"Aw, Khloe! No fair!" Lexa said. "LT's never played with us. That was a dirty trick!"

I looked over at her, confused. "Where are the deer?" I looked at both sides of the trail, not seeing any wildlife.

"There are no deer," Clare said. "Khloe just said it to try and make some of us fall."

I mock-gasped. "Khloe!"

Khloe gave me a guilty grin. "I'm sorry! I didn't even think about it."

"None of us looked, because we've played games with Khloe before and she does it all the time," Lexa said. "Clare, Drew, and I totally spaced—we should have warned you about her diabolical tricks."

I laughed. "It's okay, you guys. I fell for it. Now I get to watch."

"You should get a redo," Khloe said. "You guys want to call that a practice round?"

Everyone nodded, but I shook my head. "No way. Fair is fair. It'll be just as fun to relax"—I kicked my feet out of the stirrups—"and watch you guys play."

"You call the commands," Clare said.

"Love that," I said. "Okay. Everyone sit, then let go of your reins, drop your stirrups, and keep your horse moving with nothing other than vocal commands. If your horse stops, starts to run into another horse, or generally stops moving forward—you're out."

As much as I wanted to play, this was fun too. Everyone followed my commands.

"Hey, Lex," Clare called.

"Not listening," Lexa sang. "Can't hear you."

"Okay, but Honor might," Clare said, her voice syrupy sweet. "Honor!" She clicked her tongue against the roof of her mouth. "C'mere, girl!"

"Ooh, you guys really *play*!" I said.

"Honor," Lexa said, her voice firm. "Walk. Don't listen to Clare."

The strawberry roan mare's ears flicked back at Lexa and then swiveled toward Clare's voice.

"Honor," Lexa said again.

Drew and Khloe were oblivious to Clare's tricks. Both had their horses walking, and neither showed signs of wobbling.

Lexa kept talking to Honor, trying to keep the mare from listening to Clare's *I-have-a-treat-for-you* voice. But Honor took a step sideways, veering in front of Whisper and starting in Clare's direction.

"Sorry, Lex," I said.

Lexa shot Clare an evil eye, then winked. "We'll get you next time."

Lexa dropped back beside me.

"You make the next call," I said. "Everyone else, relax."

Lex thought for a minute. Then she called a new task.

I sat back, enjoying the battle. Whisper seemed to be watching too. This was one of the best things we'd done together in a long time.

Khloe was the next to drop out.

Clare and Drew were the only two left.

"We're about to reach the field," Khloe said, since it was her turn to decide on a command. "Last task. If no one fails in a few strides, you both win."

"You're going down, Bryant," Drew said to Clare.

"Whatever," she scoffed. "You're done and you know it."

"Swing around in the saddle to look at us," Khloe said. "And keep your horses in a straight line."

"Good one," I said.

Drew and Clare immediately dropped their reins, moved their feet out of the stirrups, and swung around to face Khloe, Lexa, and me. Both of them had the same determined look on their faces. Drew's gelding, Polo, moved forward, seeming unaffected by his rider's backward posture.

Fuego, however, sensed something wasn't right almost immediately. He twisted his head from side to side. He had no one to guide him. He didn't have Clare's eyes or reins. Before Clare could react, he started to circle back. Quickly she turned back around in the saddle and halted him.

"Great job, Drew," Clare said.

Drew smiled, settling himself back in the right direction. "You too, Clare. I think Polo's having a sleepy day, so I got lucky."

"You were both awesome," I said.

Khloe and Lexa chimed in with their congratulations. Drew modestly accepted them and caught my eye. I smiled, and he returned my gesture.

We went back to a side-by-side position and reached a grassy field. A shallow creek wound down from a hillside next to us, and water rushed over the pebbles and stones that covered the creek bed.

"This is the best trail!" I said. "It's gorgeous out here."

"We can keep walking and looking at the scenery," Lexa said, "*or* we could go for a gallop. . . ."

I glanced at her. "Do you even have to ask?"

"On three!" Khloe said. I could *feel* the excitement in her voice.

I squeezed my knees a little tighter against Whisper's sides, made sure my feet were secure in the stirrups, and leaned forward a bit. My heart pounded—adrenaline pumping.

"One . . . two . . . three!" Khloe said.

Four horses leaped forward at the same time. Dirt

changed to grass, and the hoofbeats sounded musical. Whisper matched Honor and Polo stride for stride. Each horse engaged in an immediate battle with the others. Ever and Fuego caught us. All the horses fought stride for stride—not one horse wanting to be a stride behind the other.

Whisper's gray mane blew back and she snorted, digging deeper. She found an extra burst of speed and jumped a half stride ahead. I rocked with her body, hearing only her. The horses around us disappeared. My only focus was Whisper and the feeling of her long, elegant strides covering the ground. It felt like magic.

11

AND THE OSCAR
GOES TO . . .

Lauren Towers's Blog

8:55 p.m.: Weekend wrap-up!

Yesterday was amaze! After my sleepover at R and C's on Friday night, we went on a trail ride with D. The best part was watching Whisper have fun—she *loved* getting out of her stall and not heading straight to practice. K chose a trail I'd never been on, and it was *très magnifique* (really magnificent)! The horses got to stretch their legs, especially when we let them gallop. Whisper and I *flew* over the field, and I forgot that everything else existed.

No classes.

No R.

No drama.

No thinking about home.

No missing my friends.

No thinking abt boys.

No worrying abt riding.

Just *riding*. And loving it.

When I pulled Whisper up, I was next to D. I glanced at him and was glad to be back to reality. D and I are getting closer, *very* slowly, and he seems like a guy I can trust. Plus, there's just something *so* interesting about him that I always feel like there's so much we have to talk about. So much I want to know!

After the trail ride, C, K, D, and I walked our horses back to the stable, and D and I chatted the whole way back. We went as a group to The Sweet Shoppe and got ice cream. Everyone was excited from our ride, and we started talking about the schooling show.

Oh, mon Dieu!

It's coming up faster and faster. One more weekend of practice and then . . . showtime.

Can't.

Talk.

About.

It.

Too nervous. But I will say I'm going to practice a zillion

times harder and work every spare second with Whisper. I know better than to overwork her, though, and, being with her just to talk is invaluable. I ♥ my horse. ☺

Heading to bed now. K's already snuggled in and reading a mag. I've got a copy of French *Vogue* waiting for me.

Night!

Xoxo

Posted by Lauren Towers

I closed my laptop lid and pushed back my desk chair. I unclipped my freshly showered hair and grabbed Bumble and bumble Prep and my smoothing serum from the caddy in the bathroom. Then I walked back to my bed and picked up a brush from my nightstand. Khloe had already dried her own hair and was in pjs—flowy baby-blue pants and a white tank.

Two quick knocks startled me, making me glance at Khloe and then at the door.

"No clue," Khloe said. She put down her magazine.

I opened the door to a grinning Riley. Her slinky black hair shimmered around her shoulders. She'd paired a boatneck shirt—with PINK emblazoned across the front in neon blue—with black leggings.

"Hi, *Lauren*," she said. "Can I come in for a sec?"

"Um, sure . . ."

Riley breezed by me and walked to my desk, sitting down in *my* chair. She spun it around to face Khloe, who'd sat up in bed.

"Hi, Khlo!" Riley chirped. "Read any good gossip?"

"Not really. Must be a boring week in Hollywood," Khloe said. "What's up?"

Translation: *Why are you here, Riley?*

"Omigosh, I had to come say hi to you guys!" Riley said. "It feels like I haven't seen you in foreeeevvver. It felt like I was gone a lot longer than I was."

I sat at the end of my bed, seeing Khloe's thin smile.

"Funny," Khloe said. "I thought time went by like *that*." She snapped her fingers.

Riley's smile was as fake as the sixty-carat "diamond" paperweight on my desk.

"I'm sure you all were so busy with school and riding," she said. "I'm lucky that my teachers are so generous— they're giving me extra time for my makeup work."

She covered a yawn with her hand. "I didn't have a second for homework. I barely slept!"

"Car horns and sirens too loud for you?" I asked.

Riley giggled, shaking her head. "Oh, no way. I could barely hear them. My aunt's apartment is on the Upper

East Side and on the twenty-fifth floor. I couldn't sleep because I didn't have time—I met with so many people." She put a finger to her head and looked up to the ceiling. "Gosh, I can't even remember all their names. Agents, casting directors . . ."

"Wow," I interrupted. Riley was such a brat! She had no reason to come into our room and rub her experience in Khloe's face. Not when it was Khloe's dream too. "I bet you're really exhausted." I mimicked Riley's yawn from earlier. "We were just about to go to sleep, so see you tomorrow?"

Riley stood. "Totally. I'll tell you *every* detail at lunch!"

She let herself out, and I looked at Khloe. She held up a hand as if holding a microphone. "And the Oscar for best actress in a drama goes to Khloe Kinsella for her outstanding performance in *I Don't Care What You Did in New York, Arch-Nemesis.*" Khloe bent her head in a bow and flopped back onto her pillow.

12

AND . . . ACTION!

"RILEY'S DOING AN *AWESOME* JOB OF MAKING sure *everyone* knows that she's back on campus," Khloe grumbled. "As if her 'friendly' invasion of our room last night wasn't enough."

We were walking together under Khloe's giant umbrella. It was leopard print, with cat ears that stuck up and made it the cutest umbrella I'd ever seen. It was a foggy Monday morning, and rain fell gently around us. The gray sky was full of fat, puffy clouds that threatened to burst open into a downpour at any second.

I loved rainy days—they gave me an excuse to break out my shiny apple-red rain boots. I'd done my hair in a French braid this morning to avoid looking like a giant puff ball by second period. (Thanks, Mom, for the frizzy hair gene!)

Khloe, not knowing how to French braid, had asked me to do her hair. Gladly, I'd taught her a new EBT (essential beauty trick). Now we both sported *une tresse française*.

"At least the day's half over and we've got lunch next," I said. "We can ignore Riley and enjoy free time."

I pulled open the door to the cafeteria and paused to shake off the umbrella. Khloe followed me inside. We got in the lunch line, my stomach growling.

While we waited, I glanced around and saw something that made me want to grab Khloe and drag her out of the cafeteria. Riley sat *on* a lunch table, surrounded by a group of people in our grade. Her voice carried across the cafeteria, and everyone was staring at her as if she was telling them the most amazing, groundbreaking news in history.

"What're you getting?" I asked Khloe, trying to get her attention. But I was too late. Her eyes were narrowed on Riley and her entourage.

"I'm *not* getting anywhere near that," Khloe said. "I can imagine everything Riley's saying without hearing it. It's probably the long, epic version of what she wanted to tell us last night. Sorry, not interested."

I scrunched my nose. "I'm sorry, Khlo. It just shows how classless Riley really is. There's a difference between sharing your experiences with someone and bragging about them. Sooner or later, trust me, people will get tired of the me-me-me act."

Khloe smiled. Pink princess-cut cubic zirconia earrings—a loan from me—sparkled in her ears. "You're a pretty decent best friend. Know that?"

I shrugged. "You might have said something like that once or twice."

Lunch was buffet-style today. I gravitated toward the soup and salad bar. I filled a bowl with creamed spinach and cheese soup, then threw together a salad. Romaine lettuce, cucumbers, blue cheese crumbles, grape tomatoes, a few walnuts, and raspberry vinaigrette.

Looking at the tray caught me off guard for a second. I remembered that Mom and Dad had tried unsuccessfully for *years* to get me to eat their fave salad. I'd only tried it when Becca promised I'd like it or she'd eat anything of my choosing. As an eleven-year-old, that offer had been impossible to pass up. Much to Becca's delight—her grin said *I-was-right-but-I-won't-rub-it-in-your-face*—I loved the salad. A slice of strawberry cheesecake and a Sprite and I was set.

"Ready?" Khloe asked me. She had a grilled cheese and turkey sandwich, a handful of Goldfish, and a strawberry Vitaminwater.

"Ready."

We started toward our usual table. The caf wasn't too crowded. I liked that Canterwood allowed students to eat lunch at the on-campus restaurants twice a week. Khloe said it was a new rule this year. If only Riley had chosen *today* to have pizza at the Slice.

"I want to eat as far away from *that* as possible," Khloe grumbled.

"I know it's easier said than done, but put on your poker face. Become a character, maybe, who isn't affected by Riley. If you look upset, you're giving her what she wants."

Khloe looked at me. "Go into character. You're right." She closed her eyes and inhaled through her nose. When she opened her eyes, her jaw relaxed, and there was a friendly Khloe smiling at me.

"Wow. You are seriously a *très* talented actress," I said. "I'm trying to look half as nonchalant as you do right now."

Khloe bumped her arm against mine. "You're doing a good job, and your idea was brill. Let's go!"

She'd no sooner finished her sentence when an arm shot up and waved from Riley's table. Clare stood and left the table, heading toward us. She couldn't see Riley's expression. Riley was still talking to her new posse, but her eyes were on Clare's back. Riley's nostrils actually *flared*, and a tint colored her cheeks.

"Hey!" Clare said, reaching us. She was rocking army-green skinny jeans paired with a lace-knit white cardigan over a black crewneck long-sleeved shirt.

"You know that Riley looks like she wishes she had a tranquilizer dart to shoot into your back now, right?" Khloe asked, dropping her fake act. "She wants to drag your unconscious body back to her table."

Clare *rolled her eyes.*

She didn't chew her nails.

Or look over her shoulder.

Or start backing away to head over to Riley.

"I think Riley has plenty of company for the moment," Clare said.

"Wow," I said. "I'm sorry, it's not that I didn't believe you when you said you were going to start standing up to Riley, but I didn't expect it to be like . . . well, like *this*. So soon."

"It can't be easy," Khloe said. "You can go back. I'm glad you said hi to us."

Clare shook her head. "Thanks, Khlo. I know what you're trying to do. But I'm okay. I had a long talk with Riley yesterday about how I wanted our friendship to change."

"How did she react?" I asked. People walked around us to get a table, but none of us moved.

"She didn't believe me," Clare said. "I could tell that she was thinking it was one of those times where I was just saying stuff and not going to follow through. She kept telling me to do whatever I wanted and that she didn't care. Riley *does* care, though, and I know she was sure I'd sleep on it and not do anything. So I am. Right now."

Khloe smiled. "Proud of you!"

"Thanks," Clare said. "I'm not going to ask you guys to come sit with us—I'd never do that to you, but I did want to say hey."

We talked for a few more minutes before Khloe and I headed to our table and Clare went back to her seat.

We put down our trays and sat down.

"That," Khloe said, "was the biggest move against Riley that Clare's ever made. Omigod."

"I know! I felt bad after I said it for telling Clare that I was surprised about what she'd done, but I was so shocked. She's such a quiet girl who doesn't want to upset anyone. I never expected her to really follow through with what she told us."

Khloe sipped her drink. "Maybe things are going to change around here."

"We'll see, huh?"

13

WIN

AFTER FRENCH CLASS, I HEADED TO GYM. I'D
spent a lot of time in French thinking about Clare and
Riley and Khloe. If Clare kept up her independence, I had
no idea how Riley would react. Would she drop Clare as
a friend? Retaliate against Clare? Against Khloe and me?

I stopped outside the gym doors and checked my
BBMs.

Ana:

*Happy (not!) Monday, LaurBell! Thought abt u this morning.
Mom actually let me have sugar 4 breakfast (!) & I had a blue rasp
Pop Tart. Remembered they r ur fav. Miss u.* ☹

I wrote her back.

Lauren:

Aww! Miss u 2, A! I haven't had a PT since I got here. Promise

I won't till we're eating them 2gether during break. How's everything w The Boyfriend? ☺

There was a message from Brielle, too.

Brielle:

OMG, L!! Richelle from sci is such a teacher's pet! She sits by me EVERY day (why?!) & makes me look so bad bc she answers every ? and does all this extra credit & stuff. Ugh. & this new transfer guy in English is so annoying. & it's only Mon. Boo.

Lauren:

So sry, Bri! Richelle who? Richelle Ward or Richelle Thomas? Why is Transfer Guy annoying? I know . . . feels like it's gonna b a long wk! Miss u!

I frowned and shoved my phone in my bag. That's how all of Brielle's latest messages had been. All about Yates and my ex-classmates. It wasn't that I didn't want to know about it or that she wasn't allowed to complain to me. I wanted her to ask how I was doing, though. Ana always did. Bri and Ana were very different people, but Brielle always used to BBM me to check on me if I went home after school with even a frown on my face.

In the locker room, I changed into my gym uniform— dark green shorts and a white T-shirt. Robotically, I laced up my Nikes. *You and Bri did have that awesome Skype chat,* I reminded myself. Bri had even "met" Khloe. That made me feel a little better. Bri probably thought she was making me feel better still talking about Yates as if I went there.

I closed my locker and walked to the bleachers, taking a seat with the other girls. Today it was just girls. I wished Drew had gym today so we could talk.

But at least I had forty-five minutes to work out and clear my head. I needed my Bri issues to be gone by the time I got to my riding lesson. Every second with Whisper counted. The schooling show was less than two weeks away, and there was no time to focus on anything else when I got to the stable.

"Are you okay, Lauren?"

Reluctantly I looked up at the familiar voice. Riley stood next to me, her black hair in a high, bouncy ponytail.

"I'm fine . . . thanks." I wanted to play nice if Riley was acting cool. This fresh start was important to Clare, and it would impact Khloe so much. I forced a smile. "Why did you think something was wrong?"

In the narrow space between bleachers, Riley stretched. She put one red-and-silver Reebok next to me, leaning forward to touch her fingertips to her shoe.

"Oh, you looked lost in thought or something. Must have misread you." She switched legs. "But I do want you to know that if you're worried about anything . . ." She paused, looking at me with a soft glance. "I'm here. Clare really wants to change our friendships and she's my bestie, so I want to try for her."

Whoa. Something about this was *way* too easy and fast.

"You were so mad that Khloe, Lexa, and I slept over at your place," I said. "Now you're completely over it?"

Riley sat next to me. "I was mad until I talked to Clare. Okay, and even for a little while after. But I thought about what she was *really* asking me—and you and Khloe—to do. Clare wasn't asking for us all to wear friendship bracelets and become BFFs."

I shook my head. "No, she wasn't."

"She was asking that we coexist. Be civil. Maybe it'll turn into new friendships. Maybe it won't."

"*You and Khloe* might become friends?" I asked.

Riley grinned. "Yeah, so, that one's a little less likely to happen. But Clare is my best, closest friend. If it makes her upset that we can't all be in the same room without fighting—I understand. I can't promise anything, but I'll try."

I stared at Riley. Hard. Something about this still didn't feel right. If Riley was Clare's best friend like she claimed, she would have known all this was going on.

Wouldn't she have tried to stop fighting with Khloe for Clare's sake a long time ago?

"I'm willing to try too," I said cautiously. "It will help our riding team, too, if we're all getting along."

Riley nodded. "Exactly. The show season's about to get *majorly* competitive. I mean, this schooling show seems like a teensy thing, but everyone knows it's not."

It wasn't?

"Right." I played along as if I knew what she was talking about.

"The schooling show is just a way for every rider from the surrounding schools to size up the competition. It'll give us the chance to know who to watch, who's best at what, and in return, the other riders will see who's weakest on our team."

I swept my eyes over the gym, suddenly *very* over this conversation. Where was Mr. Warren, anyway?!

"Oh, I hope I didn't make you nervous," Riley said, touching my upper arm.

I smiled, hoping some of Khloe's acting skills had rubbed off on me. "Not at all. I knew what the show was about. I'm glad we have this week, the weekend, and all of next week to practice. Plus, if we're acting like a team, we'll be that much stronger."

Riley flashed a perfect smile. "Exactly!"

Sneakers squeaked on the gym floor and Mr. Warren appeared, whistle around his neck and a basketball under each arm.

Finally.

"Good afternoon, students," Mr. Warren said. He wore his usual customized Puma tracksuit—hunter-green pants and jacket with gold stripes.

"Hi, Mr. Warren," we said.

"We're going to warm up with a few laps around the gym. I'll divide you into two teams and you'll play a short game. First team to score ten points wins."

"Do we get a prize?" a girl with sandy curls asked.

Mr. Warren smiled. "I guess I could do that. If a team reaches ten points before the period is over, then that team is dismissed and can use the rest of gym as a free period."

Cheering broke out. I *so* wanted to win!

"Get warmed up!" Mr. Warren said.

I fell in with the other girls as the eighteen of us jogged around the gym. At Mr. Warren's whistle, we changed directions. Jogging in the confined space wasn't anything like running. I sort of wished I had time to take up track.

We finished the warm-up and Mr. Warren divided us

into teams. Riley was on my team, and we huddled to discuss our plan of attack.

"My aim isn't awesome," I said. "I think I'd make a good point guard."

"Same with me," Riley said.

The rest of the girls chimed in with their thoughts, and when the whistle blew, we were ready.

Tweeeeet! Mr. Warren's whistle blew, stopping all of us where we stood. Panting, I grinned and raised my hand, slapping palms with Kelsey. She'd just made the winning basket for my team!

"Wow, ladies. I'm impressed," Mr. Warren said. "Both teams played equally hard, but Team A is the winner by two points!"

"Yay!"

"Woo-hoo!"

"Score!"

Happy exclamations came from my teammates as we hugged one another. Riley reached for me and we one-arm hugged. We'd played together on the court, guarding our shooters, and our efforts had definitely paid off.

"Nice! Free period for us!" Riley said to me.

I brushed stray, sweaty hair from my forehead. "So need it."

We hugged the girls who had to stay and went back to the locker room to change.

It didn't make sense for me to shower, since I had only one class after this before riding. I pulled out a pack of Yes to Cucumbers moist towelettes and wiped my face and neck. The scent was refreshing after gym, and I pulled a bottle of water from my bag and took a few sips.

I sat on the steps of the science building, glad Mr. Warren hadn't made Team A stay in the gym. Science didn't start for a few more minutes, so I pulled out my phone.

LaurBell: My team won in bball @ gym class! 2 bad @SwmerGuy wasn't there 2 c.

I sent the update to Chatter and opened BBM.

Lauren:

*Becs, miss u. How's ur day? *hugs big sis**

Then I clicked on Drew's name.

Lauren:

Hi. ☺ Hope ur Mon isn't 2 bad. Got out of gym early. Wish I could skip sci & go riding now.

I exited the application and scrolled through Chatter updates. *Buzz!*

A new BBM alert appeared.

Drew:

Hey! 2day's LONG. V cool abt gym. Score! I know abt wanting to skip. But we already did that once, remember? ;)

Lauren:

LOL. Kind of hard 2 4get. Sry ur day is dragging. 1 class 2 go, tho!

Drew:

I keep telling myself that. Want 2 groom & tack up 2gether?

My fingers paused over the buttons. *Type something!* I yelled at myself. Geez. He hadn't asked me to prom or something.

Lauren:

Def! Meet u @ Polo's stall?

Drew:

Sounds good. C u soon.☺

Even though I was going to see her in *five* minutes in class, I typed a message to Khloe.

Lauren:

! Drew just BBMed & asked if I wanted 2 groom & tack up 2gether b4 lesson.

I made sure the message was delivered, turned my phone on silent, and shouldered my bag. Now I couldn't wait to get to class to see Khloe and Clare and talk about Drew.

14

YOU CALL THAT
A *WARM-UP*?

"OMIGOD! JUST *GO*!" KHLOE SAID, LAUGHING. "Look at yourself!"

"What?" I asked, giggling. "I'm not doing anything. I'm waiting for you."

We'd walked back from science class to our room, and Khloe was getting ready for her lesson. I'd changed a *little* faster and was standing by the door.

"Laaaureeen."

"Um, okay." I shot her a guilty smile. "I *might* be shifting from foot to foot. And talking nonstop really fast. And asking you every two seconds if you're ready."

Khloe laughed, pulling on a T-shirt. "You managed to get dressed, brush your hair, apply gloss and deodorant, *and* unpack your backpack in the time it usually takes you to get dressed."

"So . . . ," I said coyly.

Khloe shook out her hair. "*So*, I think someone wants to be at the stable with a boy, perhaps."

I blushed. "I do. But I'm still waiting for you."

"Nope. You're going. Before I text Drew to come get you." Khloe walked over, opened the door, and gestured to the hallway. She gently pushed my shoulder. "I'll see you there! Go!"

"Okay, okay!" Laughing, I stepped into the hallway. I'd been driving poor Khloe crazy. But I knew she understood, since she'd just started seeing Zack—a *très* cute guy I'd met on my first day of school.

I forced myself to walk, not run, out of Hawthorne. *You need some time to calm down,* I told myself, *or Drew will think you've had a million cups of green tea.*

When I reached the stable area, it was already flooded with horses and riders. Each arena had someone doing something different. In the smallest arena, the beginner instructor had a group of students trotting in a circle around her. One of the arenas with dressage markers was in use by an older rider. Some students had horses tied to fence posts and tie rings, grooming them in the warm but not too hot sun.

There was no such thing as getting to the stable "early." Ever.

I picked up Whisper's tack and ducked under occupied cross-ties as I walked to her stall.

"Hi, girly!" I said as I reached Whisper.

The mare's head was over the stall door and her eyes were shut. They popped open at the sound of my voice. Whisper reached her neck toward me as I put down her tack and hurried to touch her muzzle.

"I missed you," I said. "I'm so glad to see you."

Whisper put her head over my shoulder, letting me hug her. She smelled like sweet, clean hay with a hint of the apple-cinnamon-flavored treats I gave her.

"Let me grab your stuff and we're going to meet up with Polo and Drew," I said. "Okay?"

I grabbed everything I needed and led Whisper down the aisle to Polo's stall. It was near the front of the aisle, and some of the traffic from minutes earlier had cleared. Polo's stall door opened, and Drew brought out the gelding, stopping him next to his tack trunk.

"Hey," Drew said, smiling at me.

"Hi. And hey, Polo." I reached forward and patted the blood bay's neck.

"Want to take them outside?" Drew asked. "It'll be quieter."

I nodded. "Lexa showed me a good spot."

"After you." Drew let Whisper and me in front of him. I walked to the far side of the stable, which ran along the woods. There were only a few tie rings, and no one was using them. We tied the horses' lead lines with slipknots, and I slid off the tack I'd perched on Whisper.

Drew and I started grooming, the vibe easy between us. He was wearing one of my fave colors on him—a fire-engine-red tee. The color looked amaze against his pale skin.

"I wonder what we'll work on today," Drew said. "I'm glad we're riding outside."

"Me too. There are so many things I want to work on with Whisper before the show. It feels like it's coming so fast."

"I know. But I'm glad in a way. It'll be one down. The first one of the season."

I ran a rubber curry comb over Whisper's shoulder in circles. "That's the part that scares me. The 'first' one. One minute I'm ready and can't wait to show on my horse, and the next I'm a nervous mess. *I* decided to show. No one's making me. I shouldn't be so freaked out."

"You can't control how you feel. I get why you're nervous.

But I also have seen you during lessons. You're ready."

I made sure Drew couldn't see my face while he talked. I focused on Whisper's barrel.

"Thanks," I said. "That was nice."

"Just being honest. If only you could forget it was a show and pretend it was a regular practice session."

"If only," I said, standing on tiptoes to peer over Whisper's back at him. "Practicing will help me feel better."

Drew and I ended up side by side as we curried Polo and Whisper. "If you ever want to ride together, let me know," he said.

I smiled. "I will."

"But don't ask me to ride on, say, Friday night," Drew said.

"Plans?"

"Hopefully." He picked up a dandy brush. "Interested in hitting the new Chinese place with me?"

"That sounds great! I haven't had Chinese since I got here."

"Awesome," Drew said, his blue eyes bright. "Now I've got something to look forward to this week."

"Hello, class," Mr. Conner said. He addressed the six of us lined up before him. Drew. Riley. Clare. Lexa. Cole. Me.

We greeted him. We'd gathered in the big outdoor arena, and Mr. Conner had been waiting.

"I came earlier than usual because I did not want you to warm up your horses," Mr. Conner said. "We're going to do that as a group today and work through warm-up techniques that I want to make sure you're all applying to your warm-up sessions. Warming up correctly is the best way to ensure a good performance from horse and rider, and it also lowers the chance of injury to the horse."

"Why is a proper warm-up essential?" he asked. He tucked his clipboard under his left arm, staring at us.

"It helps release tension, relaxes the horse and rider, and loosens up the horse's muscles," Cole answered.

"Good," Mr. Conner said. "A strong warm-up also benefits the rider, which we will discuss in more detail later."

"It also sort of sets the tone for the ride," Clare said. "If the warm-up doesn't go well, it can be difficult to have a good ride."

"Great addition, Clare," Mr. Conner said, nodding at her. He walked a few steps, stopping in front of Lexa. He smoothed his hunter-green polo with CCA stitched under the collar in gold thread. I wondered how many of those shirts he had.

"Not necessarily in order," Mr. Conner said, "but what

are some things a warm-up develops, Lexa? Think back to the reading I assigned last week."

Lexa licked her bottom lip. *You've got this, Lex,* I tried to channel to her.

"It helps get the horse on the aids, helps with straightness and bending, establishes contact," Lexa paused. "Oh! It also works on suppleness and balance."

Mr. Conner smiled. "Excellent."

Lexa smiled and I did too.

"Let's put all these things we discussed to work. Walk your horses to the wall, and let's run through a proper warm-up."

"This is ridic," Riley muttered, getting between Clare and me as we walked to the rail. "We're showing next weekend and Mr. Conner wants to do a *warm-up*?"

"I kind of agree," I said, my voice low. "Shouldn't we be working on technique and things we'll address in our show classes?"

"Right?!" Clare said with a slight shake of her head.

We spaced the horses along the wall—Cole first, followed by Drew, Lexa, Riley, Clare, and me.

Mr. Conner walked to the center of the arena. "In case any of you are worried," he called, "I don't expect you to find this lesson easy. If you do, please let me know."

He had supersonic hearing. No doubt about it.

"Let's begin with stretching down," he called. "I want to see your horses stretch down and round. This will encourage relaxation and roundness, and will improve contact between horse and rider."

I sat up a little straighter. This was one warm-up technique I was *not* familiar with.

Mr. Conner's eyes followed us. "When done correctly, this will teach your mount to relax through his poll, back, and neck. It'll encourage reaching for the bit, and therefore, good contact."

I gave Whisper a little more rein, but kept loose contact with my legs and didn't push her forward with my seat. She maintained a respectful distance behind Clare and Fuego. Ahead of us, the fire-colored gelding's tail swished hard at his right side. I squinted and saw that Fuego was attempting to dislodge a horsefly. Clare, looking back and down, reached with her crop and ran it over Fuego's hindquarters. Free of the fly, Fuego stopped his tail's angry back-and-forth.

Mr. Conner explained the exercise a little more, and I wished I had a voice recorder. We'd just gotten started, and it was clear that I'd underestimated what he was going to teach us today.

"When you ask your horse to stretch down, you must feel that your horse is on the aids, is moving forward with roundness in the back, and is relaxed through the neck."

"Cue your horse to continue moving forward," Mr. Conner instructed. "Use your legs rhythmically and do the same though your seat."

Whisper kept the same posture for several strides. I continued to apply the cues Mr. Conner suggested, careful not to push harder or ask for more. Whisper walked four more strides before I felt her head drop ever so slightly.

"Lauren, let your hands go with Whisper," Mr. Conner said.

I dropped my hands a little and Whisper stretched her neck, pulling the reins forward. I moved my hands with her.

"Should I give her more rein?" I asked Mr. Conner, not breaking my gaze through Whisper's ears.

"Only slightly," he answered. "If you give her too much rein, the contact will be broken."

I barely heard Mr. Conner offer suggestions to my teammates. Sweat ran down my back, and I'd never felt more focused on maintaining the contact I had with Whisper. The mare lowered and stretched her gray neck a bit more, and I allowed a small bit of rein to ease through my fingers. Whisper had never been this relaxed and connected to me during a lesson. Both of her gray ears alternated flicking back to me for instruction, all her attention on me.

"Chewing the bit is completely acceptable, Riley," Mr. Conner told her. "Adonis is doing everything you ask."

"Wonderful, everyone," he called after a few more minutes. "Now, keep up the rhythm with leg aids and your seat, but ease your horse back to a normal frame. Shorten the reins as seamlessly as possible."

Mr. Conner pushed us through warm-up techniques throughout the rest of the class. It felt more like an advanced class than a "warm-up"! When he raised his hand, signaling us to stop, every muscle in my legs, back, and arms burned. Whisper's coat had darkened from sweat and she wasn't alone—the other horses had sweated too.

"Great session, everyone," Mr. Conner said. "Cool down your horses and I'll see you tomorrow in the indoor arena. Thank you for working hard."

Our instructor headed for the exit. We all looked at one another. Mr. Conner had just left a *very* tired group of warmed-up horses and riders.

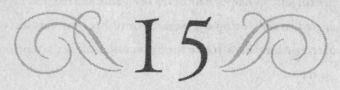

15

BE OUR GUEST

BY THURSDAY, I'D BARELY TAKEN A BREATH from school and riding. I'd just finished French and was on my way to fashion. Khloe and I hadn't seen much of each other all week. We'd done our homework together most nights and had fallen asleep before lights-out.

After riding and glee on Wednesday, we'd met up with Clare, Riley, Drew, Zack, Lexa, Cole, and Jill in one of the media center's cozy rooms to study. The precious minutes Khloe and I'd had to talk, we'd complained how we had zero time to see our guys. Khloe had *just* started dating Zack, and they'd both been too busy to go out all week.

"It's, like, life is *so* against us!" Khloe had said. "And sharing a class with him does *not* count!"

I'd agreed. At least I had my Friday date with Drew to

focus on. But by the end of the study session, Khloe had a Friday night date too! Zack had asked her out, and now Khloe and I could spend Friday evening getting ready together.

I stepped into Ms. Snow's classroom for fashion, shaking thoughts of Drew from my mind.

I sat next to Cole, my friend and partner for our upcoming project.

"You're never almost late," Cole said, his light-brown eyebrows raised. "Everything okay?"

"I lost track of time," I said. "I started thinking about all the stuff that's happened this week, and apparently, snails passed me on the way here."

Cole laughed. He slid off his gray blazer and hung it over the back of his chair, revealing a collared black button-down shirt with skinny stripes that matched the color of the blazer.

I glanced down at my own clothes: skinny jeans in need of hitting the laundry and a petal-pink capped-sleeve T-shirt.

"I feel so frumpy next to you," I said.

Cole rolled his green eyes. "Stop. You look great."

"This morning I was too tired to even care that I put on already-worn jeans."

Cole scooted his chair away from me. "Well, *that* changes things."

"Cole!"

He grinned, then laughed. He moved back over, and we giggled together.

Ms. Snow walked into the classroom. Unlike the other Canterwood teachers, she dressed to match her class. Red-bottomed Louboutins couldn't be mistaken for any other shoe. A white boatneck shirt was tucked into high-waisted flared black pants.

I wanted to *be* Ms. Snow.

Or at least share her wardrobe.

We got right to work after she called attendance.

"We've been doing lots of reading in our textbooks about costume creation and inspiration," Ms. Snow said. Her flatironed hair hit her shoulders, and the caramel highlights gave the cut dimension.

"This will hopefully be of help when you and your partner begin sketching ideas for your costume for *Beauty and the Beast*."

We hadn't been assigned costumes yet, but Cole and I had our fingers crossed for Khloe's Mrs. Potts. Khloe, however, wished we'd get Riley's Belle costume. I'd told her there was *no* way Cole and I could sabotage Riley's costume, but Khloe had insisted she'd help us come up with something if we drew Belle.

"With the seventh-grade production approaching," Ms. Snow said, "it's time to assign costumes to each pair of you. These were all a random draw, and there will be *no* trading of costumes."

A guy raised his hand. "What if we're not familiar with all the characters?"

"Good question, Alec," Ms. Snow said, smiling. "We will be viewing two versions of the play—the Disney cartoon and a staged production. I'll also be handing out information sheets to each pair with several images of the character as well as links to finding more information."

I'd seen the Disney movie too many times to count, and Cole had said he'd watched it too, so I wasn't worried that we wouldn't know a character.

Ms. Snow opened a yellow planner and began calling out names of students in our class and the character they were assigned. The characters went fast.

Maurice, Belle's father.

Gaston, the main antagonist.

Chip, Mrs. Potts's teacup son.

"The character of Belle is assigned to Kiera and Luke," Ms. Snow said.

Cole and I looked at each other. Riley's costume was gone. I'd never admit it to Khloe, but I was relieved. If we were going to keep trying to all get along, as Clare wanted, it *definitely* would not have helped for Cole and me to have been assigned Belle. The temptation to sabotage Riley's costume would have been too great.

A few more characters went.

"The costume for Mrs. Potts . . . ," Ms. Snow said.

I tensed in my seat. *Please, please, please . . .*

". . . will be done by Adriana and Lacey."

Cole and I met eyes, mouthing *no* at the same time. Major. Bummer. I'd so wanted to create Khloe's costume.

I didn't know Adriana and Lacey, but they *had* to do an amazing job. Or they'd have Khloe's BFF in their faces!

"Cole and Lauren, you will both be working on Lumière," Ms. Snow announced.

Ooh la la! I grinned and leaned over to Cole. "Lumière is my *favorite* character after Belle and Mrs. Potts!"

"Secret?" Cole said, his voice hushed. "He's my ultimate fave! I'm so glad we got him!"

We touched our palms together, and I wrote *Lumière* at the top of a new page in my notebook. Designing a new look for the famous candelabra was going to be so much fun. I was sorry not to get Mrs. Potts, out of loyalty to Khloe, but if I had to get any other character, I was glad it was Lumière.

16

IGNORANCE = BLISS

"FRIDAY, FRIDAY, FRIDAY!" KHLOE SANG, doing a little dance in our room.

I laughed. "This is the most energy you've ever had before our first class."

Khloe was brimming with energy this morning, and I was exhausted. It didn't feel like the normal worked-too-hard tiredness. My muscles hurt, and all I wanted to do was go back to sleep. But I hadn't finished my usual cup of morning green tea, and I was probably sore from the intense lessons Mr. Conner had put my team through all week.

"That, my dear best friend, is because it is Friday. Otherwise known as the last day of school in a week." Khloe's reflection in her makeup mirror smiled at me. She put on a brown-and-black feather earring. "I have more."

I stepped into black peep-toe ballet flats. "Please. Continue."

"Also, Friday is known as the day before the weekend starts. And finally, for two lucky girls in this very room, this particular Friday is date night!"

I smiled. "Indeed! Friday is the greatest day of the week per your examples."

Khloe put on her other earring and stood. "Why, thank you, LT."

"Did you and Zack decide plans yet?" I asked, walking into the bathroom. I grabbed two Tylenol and came out, then sat back on my bed. Khloe looked at the pills in my hand.

Her happy expression disappeared. "What's wrong? You okay?"

"Oh, yeah!" I said hurriedly. "I'm totally fine. My muscles are just a little sore. Riding was intense this week."

Khloe's mouth and eyes relaxed. "Okay, whew. I thought you'd hurt yourself or something." She stood in front of the mirror, smoothing her black V-neck with ruffled sleeves and adjusting the pink belt on her jeans.

"No, not at all. I'll be completely fine once I take these." I tossed the pills into my mouth and washed them down with tea. I finished what was in my cup and waited for the caffeine to kick in.

"I understand the soreness," Khloe said. "The back of my calves are, like, *I hate you!* right now. Mr. Conner keeps saying 'schooling show,' but he's making us practice as if we're going to regionals or something."

"I'm complaining now," I said, trading places with Khloe to stand in front of the mirror, "but I'm relieved the workouts are so intense. The last thing I want is to be unprepared."

I checked my reflection in the mirror. I wore a pair of Khloe's whiskered jeans with one of my favorite shirts—a sky-blue cotton tee with a white heart in the center. I'd accessorized with thin silver hoop earrings and my beryl birthstone necklace.

Khloe put her bag over her shoulder. "With Mr. Conner as your coach, the last thing you'll ever be is 'unprepared.' Trust me."

I grabbed my own bag. It felt a lot heavier than I remembered when I packed it last night. *You need to hit the gym and start lifting weights,* I told myself. Together, Khloe and I left Hawthorne for English class.

Despite my excitement about tonight with Drew, the day dragged.

And dragged.

And dragged.

My backpack seemed to get heavier and heavier after each class. No shock, since teachers always loaded us down with homework for the weekend, but I had to keep putting it down and picking it back up.

The Tylenol never kicked in, and I made a big effort to keep up with my friends as we went from class to class. But any time I had a class alone, I walked so slow, I was almost late.

I downed two Diet Cokes at lunch but didn't feel any more awake than I had this morning. Plus, the soda was the only "lunch" I had. Nothing sounded good. Not even the tomato cheddar soup that I'd usually almost run people over to get.

Khloe and Lexa had asked, repeatedly, if I felt okay during lunch. I'd said I wasn't hungry and had grabbed a bag of chips between classes. They'd seemed to sort of accept my answer and then had gotten distracted talking about the e-mail Mr. Conner had sent, canceling all intermediate and advanced riding lessons for the afternoon. I wanted to be upset about the loss of a practice session, but I couldn't. Getting through a lesson didn't seem possible with my stomach churning and waves of nausea hitting me at random intervals.

Even now, walking back to Hawthorne after my last class of the day, I didn't want to admit it out loud. If I said it, it could come true. I could say it in my head, though.

I think I'm sick.

But if I ignored how I felt, took more Tylenol, and drank white tea—which was packed with antioxidants—I'd feel better before I even got truly sick.

"There," I said, closing my door behind me. "That's a plan. No need to panic."

Saying it aloud didn't stop my nerves. I couldn't get sick! Any other time—fine. But not now. Not when I needed every day in the arena to practice with Whisper before the show. Not when I needed to be attending every gym class and keeping myself in shape for the schooling show.

I dropped my backpack by my desk and went into the bathroom. With one eye closed, I peeked at my face in the mirror.

Uh-oh.

My fair cheeks were flushed a light pink. I touched my forehead. Warm. Not hot, though. If Khloe asked about my cheeks, I could tell her I'd gotten carried away with blush. I changed out of my school clothes into comfort clothes—an old sweatshirt, tank top, and lounge pants.

I made myself a cup of white pear tea in the common room and downed it. I found the bottle of multivitamins that Mom had sent (and I'd yet to open) in the bathroom cabinet. I took one and two more Tylenol. Hopefully, the vitamins and tea would stop whatever I was getting before it really started. I'd even call it an early night with Drew to get to bed and, fingers crossed, wake up feeling *perfect*.

17

CAKE ON THE MAKEUP

I'D JUST PUT AWAY THE TYLENOL WHEN Khloe walked in. Her tan cheeks were flushed, and she had an extra bounce in her step. Khloe was always animated, but this was her going-on-a-date bouncy. I smiled, despite how I felt.

"Are you *so* ready to start date prep?" she asked.

"Ready," I said, making sure to sound normal and not on the verge of s-i-c-k. "Drew and I are grabbing Chinese, and our plans are up in the air after that. We'll decide after dinner."

"That sounds awesome. You guys have a million possibilities for tonight."

Nodding, I sipped the ginger ale I'd gotten from the common room and poured into a plastic glass. I just didn't

want Khloe to know how I felt. She was my best friend—
she'd worry. Plus, she was so excited about her date with
Zack. I didn't want to bring down her night. It was *so* rare
that we had free time lately with practice and school. I
really did want to have fun tonight—starting with date
prep with Khloe and then seeing Drew.

We sat at our desks and opened our three-way makeup
mirrors. We turned on the mirror lights, and I laid out
my makeup. I looked in the mirror, and tiny dots of
sweat had popped up along my hairline. My cheeks had
reddened.

I sneaked a glance at Khloe—her back was to me. *Whew.*
A finger to my cheek confirmed what I already knew. I had
a fever. No. No. No. I couldn't be sick!

Not now.

Not when the show was next weekend.

Not when I had classwork to do.

Not when I had a date with a boy I liked.

Stop whining. You showed in a three-day event when you had the
flu and nobody *found out. It's just a tiny fever. You can hide this*
until it goes away. Which it totally will.

I sat up straighter in my desk chair and pulled out a
face wipe. The cooling wipe soothed my face, and I pulled
off my sweatshirt. The air felt good on my bare arms. My

face was going to require a little, okay, a *lot* more makeup than usual to cover my fever.

"Zack has been so cute about today," Khloe said. "He texted me a rose emoticon and said it was my pre-date gift."

"Aw!" I said, working fast to spread ivory foundation over my cheeks. I *never* wore foundation, but I had to. There was no way Khloe would let me out of the room with flaming cheeks.

"The best part," she said, starting to laugh, "was that Zack added that an *emoticon* rose was the lamest 'gift' ever and he hoped I didn't expect that all future gifts from him would come through BBM."

I laughed too, my stomach lurching a little. "I'm so glad you two are going out," I said. "He's like you in a lot of ways—funny, silly, smart. And he seems like a good guy."

"He is," Khloe said. She held an eyelash curler over her right eye.

"Zack better be. All the time to my BFF. Or I will do more than send him an emoticon with a black eye."

We giggled together. I smoothed the Covergirl foundation, blending it along my jawline. It covered my freckles—something I wasn't used to seeing. I curled my lashes, starting to feel a little better, and applied a light coat of brown mascara on my upper lashes. The ginger ale had helped the nausea, and the Tylenol had finally started to work.

I smiled to myself. Maybe I had caught it just in time. I peered in the mirror, looking *very* closely at my face. Why hadn't the foundation covered the red? It didn't even look as though I'd applied blush. It looked like I'd spent a weekend at the Hamptons without sunblock.

I fumbled through my makeup, grabbing a cover-up stick. I rubbed the heavy makeup on my cheeks.

There.

Redness gone!

I'd have to come up with an excuse for why I was wearing so much (too much) makeup, but at least I'd covered the fever. Just to be safe, I patted powder on my cheeks. Clear gloss, and makeup was done.

Staying at my desk, I ran a brush through my hair, deciding to let it stay loose and wavy tonight.

I turned my chair and went to my closet. "Makeup done," I said. "Now clothes. You know it's code that you've got to help me choose."

"Of course," Khloe said. "And I'm not setting one foot outside the door without fashion advice from Lauren Towers."

I looked through my shirts, ignoring that the fact that *everything* started hurting the second I'd stood.

"I'm flattered," I said. "You know the way to my heart." Grinning, I turned to her, a hand over my chest.

Khloe smiled, and I turned back to my clothes.

"Um . . . Laur?"

"Yeah?" I asked.

"Did you totally change your makeup routine?" Khloe asked. "I didn't pay attention to how you did yours tonight. Did I miss a huge EBT?"

I kept my gaze on my clothes, pretending to be concentrating on a shirt. "You didn't miss anything at all. I added extra cover-up because I had some really gross breakouts that came out of nowhere. Perf timing, right?"

"Ugh, I hate when that happens. I always break out at the 'ideal'—*not*—moments. Thank whoever invented Clearasil! An invention that has saved countless people from going into hiding when a monster pimple popped up."

I wanted to laugh, but I couldn't. My eyes watered nonstop, and I swallowed saliva. And kept swallowing. I took a huge breath through my nose and sat on the chair next to my closet, forcing myself to focus on the shirts I'd picked. By "picked," I meant grabbed before another bout of nausea hit.

"I can't wait to hear what you think about the Chinese place," Khloe said. "It's about time we got Chinese on campus. Cold noodles with sesame sauce, kung pao chicken, and orange chicken are my ultimate faves."

I squeezed my eyes shut and blew a big breath through my mouth. Hot and cold swept over my body, almost at the same time. Just the *mention* of that food—I couldn't even think about the specifics—had me five seconds away from running into the bathroom. The ginger ale that had tasted good moments earlier rose in my throat. I sat absolutely still. Our room felt like a boat on rough waters and I was seasick.

"Lauren."

The tone of Khloe's voice made me open my eyes. Slowly.

"Need help with something?" I managed to get out, trying to keep my voice casual.

"I really do," Khloe said. "I'm trying to figure out why my roomie looks like she's about to throw up and isn't telling me."

My shoulders slumped. I leaned forward, the shirts falling, and clutched my stomach.

Khloe was kneeling beside my chair in an instant, a hand on my arm. "Laur, what's going on? Please tell me so I can help."

"Nauseous," was all I could say.

"You're doing the right thing. Keep your head down and stay still." Khloe switched from date mode to in-total-control mode in a millisecond. "If you feel like the room's spinning or you're dizzy, shut your eyes, too."

"'Kay," I whispered. White spots swam in front of my closed eyes.

"Do *not* move. I'm going to the bathroom to get a cold washcloth. I'll be right back."

I heard Khloe's bare feet hurry across the floor, and she muttered at the water to come out faster.

She knelt back beside me. I still had my eyes closed, but I felt her knee brush my foot. She put a cozy blanket over my now shivering shoulders, and I wrapped it over my arms and across my chest. I heard the mini-fridge door open, and a soda can popped open. Khloe brought over a ginger ale with a straw and PeptoBismol tablets.

I lifted my head slightly, opened my eyes, and took small sips and chewed the tablets. Khloe stayed beside me while I waited to see if the medicine would help. After a few minutes, the nausea lessened enough for me to talk.

"Thank you. I'm so sorry, Khloe. I—"

"Shhh. Not right now." Khloe's brown eyes were wide with concern. "Just listen to me. If you're able to sit up all the way, and you can keep your eyes closed if it helps, I'll put a cool washcloth on your forehead. It'll help with the nausea."

I stayed bent over, taking a breath.

"You're going to be fine, Laur. Promise. Lots of things could have made you feel sick all of a sudden. You skipped lunch, so you might be really, really hungry. Or if you had a snack, maybe it upset your stomach. It might be something that goes away just like *that*."

I slowly raised my head. Khloe was going to find out about my fever the second she touched my forehead.

"Good job," she said, her voice soothing. "Does anything else feel wrong?" She held the pink washcloth, ready to apply it to my forehead.

I reached for the washcloth and swiped it across my cheeks. One at a time.

"Omigosh, Lauren!" Khloe said, touching my blanket-covered arm. "You have a fever! It looks like a bad one. Oh, no."

"Please let me apologize this time. Khlo, I felt sick all day. I thought if I ignored it, then it would go away. I really thought I was sore from riding when I took the Tylenol this morning, but I kept feeling worse and worse."

"You should have left class and gone to the nurse," Khloe said. Her tone wasn't judgmental, just sad.

"I couldn't. I didn't want to even think about the possibility that I was, okay, *am* sick. I can't be sick now. There's so much going on. I can't miss one day at the stable, and I was so excited about tonight for both of us. I'm ruining it now."

"No," Khloe's voice was firm. "You're not. Did you choose to get sick? *No.* I get why you didn't want to believe it. But you're sick, Laur."

She put a hand to my forehead. "Oh. I'll get Christina after we get you into bed. You must feel awful. Poor LT." She took the washcloth from my hand and pressed it lightly to my forehead.

"That feels really good," I said, tilting my head back a little. "I'm so sorry I didn't tell you. I really thought I could make it through a date with Drew and sleep off whatever this is. That's why I'm wearing ten pounds of foundation. I'm *really* sorry I lied to you about that. I hoped I could cover the redness from the fever."

Khloe was quiet for a minute. "I'm most upset that you have clear skin without the hint of a breakout in sight. When I apply concealer, it's to cover *real* zits! I hate you a little for that."

I laughed a little, even though it hurt my stomach. "You're being so wonderful about this."

Khloe stuck out her bottom lip. "I don't like it when my best friends are sick."

"Oh, Khlo! You need to leave! Zack! Your date!" I uncovered an arm and took the washcloth. "Tell him it's my fault you're late. I'm just going to crawl into bed and sleep."

"Wow, your fever must be insanely high. There's no way I'm leaving you alone while you're sick."

"Khloe," I said. Nausea bubbled in my stomach. "You have to go. You were so excited."

"I was. But guess what? There's a Friday night *every* week. I'd be worrying about you the entire time. Please don't feel bad or like it's your fault. I *want* to stay and help take care of you in any way I can."

"You're—you're amazing. I—"

I dropped the washcloth, covered my mouth with my hand, and ran for the bathroom. The blanket fell off me during my dash to make it. I got on my knees in front of the toilet and had barely lifted the lid and seat before throwing up.

"Coming in," Khloe said softly.

She gathered my hair and put it in a loose ponytail.

She sat on the bathtub edge, a hand on my back. "You poor thing. It's going to be okay. I'm right here unless you tell me to go."

I shook my head from the toilet. Khloe gave me a handful of toilet paper. I'd just finished wiping my mouth when I started throwing up again.

18

SICK. AWESOME.

WHILE I CURLED INTO A BALL ON THE BATH-room floor after the umpteenth time of throwing up, Khloe went to get her phone.

"I'm texting Lexa to get Christina," she said. "No way I'm leaving even just to go down the hallway."

I nodded, pressing my hot cheek against the cool tile. I'd never felt this sick. Ever. Not even when I'd gotten food poisoning a few summers ago from mayonnaise on sandwiches at a picnic.

Someone knocked on our door and then opened it.

"Oh, no, Lauren," Christina said, coming into the bathroom. "Aw, sweetie." She sat beside me and lightly rubbed my back. "We're going to get you feeling better. I'm so sorry you're sick."

"Thank you for coming over," I said, my voice barely audible.

I shut my eyes again, feeling like I was going to throw up.

Khloe told Christina everything that had happened since we'd been in the room together and mentioned the parts I'd told Khloe about how I'd felt during the day. I listened to them, feeling as though I was drifting in and out of a fog.

"I don't want Lauren sleeping on the bathroom floor," Christina said to Khloe. "Let's get her into bed. Don't try to move her until I get a bowl to put beside her in case she gets sick again."

"I'll be right back, Laur," Christina said.

I fell asleep on the floor before she returned.

19

WORLD'S #1 BFF

WHEN I WOKE UP, IT WAS STILL DARK EXCEPT for Khloe's unicorn night-light. She was propped up in her bed, a magazine on her chest, sound asleep.

The alarm clock read 4:44 a.m. I tried to remember the haze of last night. Christina and Khloe had helped me into bed, covering me with cool sheets and adding an extra blanket on top of my comforter.

Christina had put a red plastic bowl next to me. I'd heard her tell Khloe that she would be in every couple of hours to check on me, but if Khloe needed anything to call her no matter what time.

Khloe.

She had gone above and beyond a BFF. All night she'd given me sips of water and ginger ale, rinsed out my bowl if I'd gotten sick, and changed the washcloth on my forehead.

"I'll stay up all night with you, Laur," she'd told me despite my weak protests.

The last time I'd looked at the clock had been sometime after two in the morning, so my bestie hadn't had much sleep at all.

I vaguely remembered Christina coming in and out and taking my temperature every so often.

I wanted to tell Khloe to snuggle under her own covers and get comfortable, but I also didn't want to wake her. But before I could decide what to do, I fell asleep again.

20

WHERE DID THE
WEEKEND GO?

"I CANNOT BELIEVE IT'S SUNDAY NIGHT," I said. "I slept almost all weekend!" I adjusted the pillow behind me.

"As you should have," Khloe said. "You have the flu, Laur. You needed the rest."

"*Had* the flu," I said. "Had. I'm not throwing up or nauseous anymore. Plus, my fever's gone."

Khloe, sitting on her bed, gave me a Mom-like look. "I'm so, so glad all that's gone. But you haven't kept down any food until the chicken soup you had for lunch today. You're still going to need rest and time to recoup."

I nodded. "Oh, I'll get plenty of rest tonight. Going to bed early will help. Then I'll take it easy through classes tomorrow so I don't wear myself out before I get to my lesson."

Khloe got up and sat at the end of my bed. She was in her fave pair of zebra print pjs—a cami and shorts. "Laur, Christina's not going to let you go to class tomorrow. She came in a little while ago when you were asleep and said she'd let all your teachers know you'd be out tomorrow."

"What?" I shook my head. "No, I'm fine to go to class. Christina doesn't know how much better I feel. Once I tell her, she'll let me go."

Khloe looked at her lap, then at me. "I know you. You want to get back to everything. But if you push it, you'll get really sick all over again. Christina's mind is set—trust me."

"But Khloe, if I don't go to class, then I won't be allowed to ride! We have lessons tomorrow!"

"Ugh. I *hate* telling you this. I'm sorry, Lauren, but Christina told Mr. Conner how sick you were, and they decided you couldn't ride tomorrow."

Anger replaced the hot feeling of the fever I'd felt in my body all weekend. "That's not fair. I didn't get to ride at *all* this weekend. I missed two entire days of riding! Now Mr. Conner won't let me ride tomorrow? We have a show on Saturday."

I folded my arms, throwing myself back into my pillows.

"I'd be mad too. Maybe try to think of the positive? You get to skip school tomorrow and sleep, watch TV, or do whatever you want. You'll get rested up, and you'll come back to the stable in perf shape."

"Missing three days of riding because of being sick and then forced to rest isn't going to help me *or* Whisper at all," I said. "She's used to being exercised almost every day."

"I know Mike and Doug took turns exercising her this weekend," Khloe said, her tone soft. "If it would make you feel better, I could work her tomorrow. Only if you want, obviously."

I knew I was acting like a brat, but I didn't care. It felt like no one understood how important practicing was for the schooling show. But Khloe wasn't the bad guy. She'd taken care of me all weekend. She'd skipped her date with Zack and had texted Drew, too, to let him know I was sick. Drew had written a sweet BBM that he was sorry I was sick and to let him know if I needed anything. Now Khloe was only trying to help.

"I'd love for you to ride Whisper if you have time," I said. "That would mean a lot. Thank you."

"Of course," she said. "I get why you're mad and frustrated. I really do. I'm sorry you got sick and that it cut into your practice time. But just think—when you *do* get in the arena, you'll be feeling great and you'll make triple sure every second counts."

I half smiled. "Yeah. I guess so."

Khloe took a breath. "Try not to get down. I know that's easy to say, but you're ready for the show. If you didn't have a chance to practice again before riding in your classes, you'd do great."

I opened my mouth.

"I'm not saying any of that just because we're friends," Khloe said, stopping me before I could argue. "I'm saying it because it's true. You're ready for your trail and dressage class. Zero doubt in my mind."

"Thanks, Khloe. I don't feel that way, honestly, but your support means so much. Everything you did for me this weekend—I'll never be able to thank you enough. I wouldn't be as well as I am if you hadn't taken care of me."

Smiling, Khloe went back to her own bed. I stared at the TV, not even hearing the words. Even though Khloe believed in me, I didn't. I needed to be in the arena. I was jealous of Khloe and everyone else who rode this weekend and would get to practice tomorrow.

Christina had insisted that Khloe get some air on Saturday and Sunday afternoon, so she had worked out with Ever. I hated that I felt envious that Khloe had been able to ride and I hadn't. It was so immature! She deserved to do whatever she wanted in the whole two hours she'd spent out of our room this weekend. Plus, I'd put her at major flu risk. Thankfully, she showed no signs of being sick.

I still couldn't stop the anxiety about all the lost riding time. Whisper and I needed the practice as much as anyone, and we'd missed two days and were on schedule to miss a third. I'd had my stable time for the entire weekend and week planned. Now the only place the schedule belonged was in the trash.

21

BLUR OF A WEEK

THE WEEK PASSED IN A BLUR. I'D SLEPT ALL day Monday, proving the point that I *did* need the rest. When Khloe had gotten back from riding, I'd woken up feeling better.

Really, *really* better.

Khloe had filled me in about her exercise with Whisper, and the mare had behaved like a pro. Even though I'd still felt upset about not riding, I was grateful that Whisper got a workout with my friend.

I'd felt strong enough to go to the dining hall that night and have dinner. The walk to the caf, though, had exhausted me, and I'd fallen asleep moments after we came back to our room.

Christina decided I could try a half day of classes on

Tuesday if I truly wanted to go. I'd gone and turned in my makeup work. It had felt great to see my friends—especially Lexa and Clare, who'd been BBMing me the entire time I was sick. I e-mailed Mr. Conner to tell him how I was feeling, and he wrote back that I could groom Whisper, but no riding until Wednesday. For a second, I'd started to compose an e-mail begging him to let me ride. Then I deleted the words I'd written and instead thanked him and said I couldn't wait to be back in the stable. My anger at not being allowed to ride melted away at that moment. Mr. Conner had gotten Whisper and me this far. It was only fair that I trust him in return.

Wednesday was when I'd *really* lost track of time. I rushed through school on Wednesday and Thursday to get to the stable. Both lessons had been tough, but Whisper hadn't given me any problems. She acted as if she'd encountered the trail-class obstacles a dozen times before when I'd ridden her through the course. I'd been too tired to even pay attention to Riley.

Dressage had been nearly as flawless. Thanks to workouts from Mike, Doug, and Khloe, Whisper acted as if no time had been lost. When I'd finally come up for air, it was Friday afternoon. The day before our schooling show.

22

ONE DAY TO GO

"YOU'RE PROBABLY WONDERING WHY I'VE gathered the intermediate and advanced teams," Mr. Conner said. "I e-mailed each of you requesting that you come without your horse, because this afternoon will be a bit different."

Standing together, Khloe, Clare, Riley, Drew, Lexa, and I looked at one another.

"There will be no intermediate or advanced lessons today," Mr. Conner continued. "I want your horses to rest. We, on the other hand, have guests coming. The stable reflects our team. Therefore, I want it to be in perfect condition."

"Ugh, cleaning," Khloe whispered.

"You'll each be assigned a few stable chores. Everyone

must clean his or her tack in addition to whatever else you're given to do." Mr. Conner smiled at us. "When the stable passes inspection, you can leave. I want this to be an early night for you, so please come to me for your assignments and get started."

Riders started lining up. Clare, Khloe, Lexa, and I got into line, and I spotted Drew way ahead of us. He waved, and I smiled back.

"Riles, come on," Clare said, waving at her friend.

Her roommate hadn't moved. Instead there was a weird look on her face, and her feet seemed cemented to the ground.

"Riley?" Clare said. "Come on. We have to do these chores so we can get out of here."

Riley waved her hand. "*You* guys have to do chores. I'm leaving now."

"You can't get out of helping," I said.

"Yeah, we *all* have to stay," Khloe said, anger in her voice.

Riley stepped over to us, looking into Khloe's eyes. She paused, putting her hand on her hip. "I got the job in New York."

Wait. *What?!*

"Ha-ha. Very funny," Lexa said.

Clare stared at Riley. One look at Riley's face and I knew it was true.

"When did you find out? You didn't even tell me," Clare said. Her voice shook.

"And why would I tell you, Clare? You've made new friends. You tried to force *me* to be friends with them. I knew when I got back to Canterwood that I had the part."

Silence. No one had a response. I was too shocked to think of anything to say.

"The whole 'of course I'll try to get along with your loser friends?' It's called *acting*," Riley said. "I had to keep practicing somehow."

"You are a horrible person," Khloe said, her face red. "I don't care that you got a job. I don't care that you played all of us. I *do* care that you hurt Clare. She's supposed to be your best friend!"

Riley shrugged. "Was my best friend. Now she's all yours. And so is the part of Belle. You got everything you wanted, Khloe! Congratulations."

I held myself back from getting in Riley's face. She wasn't worth it.

"My stuff is being moved out of our room now," Riley said to Clare. "I'll be gone by the time you finish your chore fest. I only came to this meeting to see all of you at once. Watch for me on TV!"

She turned, her black hair swishing around her shoulders, and disappeared.

Not one of us moved except to shuffle forward in line. No one said her name. It was done. Riley Edwards was no longer a student at Canterwood Crest Academy.

Back in our room, Khloe and I took turns showering and getting ready for bed. On our walk back to Hawthorne, we'd made a pact not to talk about Riley until after the show. We knew we'd talk about it *forever*, and it would take away too much of our focus. We had, however, made sure Clare was okay. She'd promised she was and that she'd text if she needed us. I couldn't imagine what she was going through—losing a best friend. And the night before a show. But something told me that Clare wasn't too down. That Riley's departure had set her free somehow.

It was going to be an early night, but I felt wired. Images of my last show—of Red Oak—kept threatening to explode in front of me. I tried to keep busy, doing anything to occupy my mind.

My phone buzzed, and I opened BBM.

Taylor:

Wanted to say GOOD LUCK, Laur. Even tho u so don't need it.

Lauren:

Thank you! I'm nervous, but I trust Whisper.

Taylor:

Not worried abt u 2 @ all. Wisp is UR horse. R u excited 2 show her off?

Lauren:

Definitely!! Cross ur fingers 4 me that I do CC proud.

Taylor:

I will, but u don't need luck.

Lauren:

What r u doing?

Taylor:

Wish I could say something cool. But just playing Wii @ home.

Lauren:

Aww! I miss that! I kicked ur butt @ Mario Kart EVERY TIME.

Taylor:

Excuse me? You must be mistaking me 4 someone else.

Lauren:

LOLOL. Fiiine. Just wait till I c u on break. . . .

Taylor:

Can't wait. Let me know how 2mrw goes!

Lauren:

I will! TTYL!

Taylor wasn't my boyfriend anymore, but he *was* my friend. It meant a lot to me that he'd remembered the show and messaged me.

"Want to get out our clothes for tomorrow?" Khloe asked.

"Sure," I said. Since we'd been back in our room, Khloe had been amazing. She hadn't said anything yet, but I knew she sensed my nerves. She'd kept me distracted with gossip, TV, and stories about *Beauty and the Beast* rehearsal this week.

We went to our closets, and I looked through my stack of show breeches.

"Tan or black?" I asked.

"I'm going with tan," Khloe said. "Easier to hide Ever hair."

"Good point," I said. "Whisper's hair isn't exactly easy to keep hidden on black breeches."

I put my newest pair over my arm. The schooling show's dress code wasn't strict like regular shows. Mr. Conner had told us we could skip jackets, ties, pins, and the rest of the usual show attire as long as we wore appropriate tops.

"I'm thinking *this*," I said. Khloe turned to me as I held up a light-blue button-down dress shirt that I'd normally wear under a show jacket.

"Perfect," Khloe said. "It'll go gorgeous with your eyes."

"Thanks!" I smiled. "And you?"

She rifled through a few shirts in her closet before pulling out a crisp navy blouse. "This one?"

"Love it. The dark blue will stand out with your light hair."

"Win. Thanks, LT."

We each grabbed zip-up hoodies to cover our show shirts while we got our horses ready in the morning. Neither of us wanted to run back to Hawthorne for a clean shirt if Whisper or Ever decided to use one of us as a Kleenex.

We hung up our clothes on the outside of our closets. I took my show boots—already polished—from their bag in the closet and put them and socks by the door. Khloe did the same.

"I'm setting the alarm for four," she said. "That sound right?"

"Our first classes are at eight . . . add time to get dressed, groom, tack up, warm up, extra time for anything crazy—yep, four is perfect."

Khloe set her alarm clock on her nightstand and I did the same. I even set my phone alarm. There was no such thing as too many backups on show day.

"I've got to take off my nail polish," Khloe said, holding up her hand. Her nails were neon orange.

"Good idea." My own nails were bare. I'd skipped painting them this week. I knew it would be a waste of polish—I'd just peel the polish off whenever I got anxious. "I'm going to see if Ana or Brielle are around to talk for a few minutes."

Khloe smiled. "Everything's going to be fine tomorrow, Laur. Better than fine. I know you're scared, but I'm not worried about you. Brielle and Ana are going to say the same."

I picked up my computer and sat on my bed with it in my lap. "Thanks, Khlo. You may not be worried about me, but I am. This is my first show with Whisper. I don't want to let her down. Or myself."

"You won't." Khloe's tone was firm. She picked up a bottle of polish remover from her nightstand and grabbed cotton balls from the bathroom.

I put my hands on top of my computer, trying to take even breaths to keep my heartbeat from speeding up. "What if I wake up tomorrow and freeze? What if I don't even make it to the arena? What if I somehow got sick so I couldn't show? I could have backed out."

Khloe sat in the center of her bed with her back against the wall so she was looking directly at me.

"Did you?" she asked.

"No. You know I'm showing tomorrow."

"Okay, so you didn't 'somehow' give yourself the flu and pull out."

I twisted my necklace. "I'm so afraid that I'll mess up and use the days I couldn't ride as an excuse."

Khloe soaked a cotton ball with pink-tinted polish remover. "What do you mean?"

"If I bomb in every class," I said, "I'm afraid I'll tell myself it was because I missed practice during the days I was sick. But the real truth is probably that I wasn't ready to show in the first place. That the outcome would have been the same no matter how much practice time I had. " I paused, trying to breathe.

"You know you're ready." Khloe put heavy emphasis on each word. "You know it in your gut. Laur, you got sick for a lot of reasons. You were exhausted and run-down. You *were* and are stressed about tomorrow. Who knows—maybe it was none of those things and you caught a random bug." She paused, staring hard at me.

"I—"

She shook her head and kept going. "But not one of those reasons was because you somewhere in your deepest subconscious wanted to get sick, magically contracted the flu, and gave yourself an out to either scratch from the show or use it later as an excuse if you needed it."

I stared at Khloe for a minute, digesting everything she'd said. "Khloe," I finally said, "I don't know what to say. You said all the right things. I *am* so nervous about tomorrow, but I want to do it. I never wanted to get sick— I hated every second of it."

"I know. I was here. Don't tell me how I almost had to lock you in our room to keep you from sneaking into the stable with a hundred-and-one-degree fever."

We smiled at each other. I giggled. "If I'd gotten past you and Christina, I'd probably have gotten lost in my fever haze and ended up at the steps of Blackwell or something crazy."

Khloe laughed. "Oh, puh-lease. It wouldn't be an accident if you ended up at *Drew's* dorm."

Grinning, I rolled my eyes. "Maybe not on a normal day. But sick, gross Lauren would definitely not have wanted Drew to see her all sweaty and germy."

"Point," Khloe said.

"Thanks, Khlo," I said softly.

"Go make yourself a cup of tea before you do anything else," she said. "That's an order."

I saluted. "Yes, ma'am. I couldn't have come up with a better idea myself."

Khloe went to work on her nails. I picked up my phone from the end of the bed. Before I went to the common room, I opened BBM and typed a message to Ana, then copied and pasted it to Brielle.

Lauren:

U around? Meet me on IM to talk in 5? Rlly nervous abt 2mrw.

I pushed aside my computer and left my phone on the bed. Khloe didn't want anything from the common room. I put on black slippers with multicolored hearts and walked down the hallway. Lights blazed under doorways and music streamed softly from some rooms. Others were quiet, with nothing but the glow and faint sound of a TV. Some had no lights or TV.

I entered the common room, and a few girls from the second floor were sprawled in front of the TV, watching a horror flick. A zombie staggered across a field, chasing a limping girl. *Not* my genre at all! I couldn't even watch silly horror movies that most people giggled over, because the fake blood was so bad. I smiled at the girls, one with a blanket pulled almost over her eyes, and kept my own gaze off the TV.

I put just enough water in the teakettle for one cup of tea so it would boil fast. From the cabinet next to the stove, I took out my white mug with a hot-pink heart on it. A packet of Splenda went into the cup, and I grabbed my tea box. Something ultra-calming was a necessity. While the water heated, I went back and forth between two Celestial Seasonings teas: Sleepytime and Honey Vanilla Chamomile. Finally I settled on my first instinct—Sleepytime—because it had a mix of herbs that would hopefully calm my semi-upset stomach.

"Ahhh!" a girl screamed suddenly.

I jumped at the sound, and my hand swung over the counter, knocking over a metal napkin holder. The girl who had screamed now had her head completely covered by the blanket.

"Zara!" Another girl paused the movie and yanked the blanket off her friend—presumably Zara. "Other people *are* in here! You totally scared that girl in the kitchen."

Zara, brushing black bangs out of her eyes, looked up at me from her spot on the floor. She blushed. "Sorry! I'm such a wimp about these movies. I didn't mean to scare you."

"It's totally okay," I said, righting the napkin rack. "I couldn't even watch the screen when I came in. I'm so scared of horror movies—I probably would have screamed from here if I'd looked."

Zara smiled. "As part of my apology, we'll keep it paused until you're done."

"Oh, no way. That's so nice, but keep watching. I don't want to stop your movie."

The other girls shook their heads. "We can wait a minute," said the brunette holding the remote. "It'll be good for Zara. We really like her, and it wouldn't be the *best* thing ever if she had a heart attack."

I laughed with the rest of the girls. "Okay. But only because we don't want the common room to be invaded by EMTs."

The teakettle whistled, and I turned off the burner. Steaming water went into my cup, and I turned off the light.

"Have fun," I said to the girls on my way out.

"If you hear ambulance sirens, you know the movie was too much for Zara," one of the girls said, laughing. Zara stuck out her tongue.

Giggling, I left the common room and went back into my room. Khloe looked up at me when I came in. I told her about Zara and the movie, making her face red with laughter.

My phone blinked. There were BBMs from Ana and Brielle.

Ana:

Online! Here 4 u, LT! ♥

Brielle:

Get logged on!!

I opened my laptop, woke it up, and logged into IM.
I snuggled under my covers while I waited for my log-in
to finish.

Brielle and Ana were both there.

Laur♥:

Hiiii, guys!!

ItsAna:

LT! Hi, B!

Bri~xo:

Lauren! Hey, Ana!

Laur♥:

*I'm so glad u were avail 2 chat. I rlly needed 2 hear from my
best friends rite now.*

ItsAna:

Of course we'd be here 4 u. Tmrw's a big day. Talk 2 us.

Bri~xo:

*I'm rlly glad u BBMed us, L. If we didn't hear from you, A and
I had already decided 2 call.*

Laur♥:

Ur such good friends. I can't stay up late. But I can't sleep, either. I'm so nervous. Keep seeing Red Oak. Skyblue. The ambulance. Ugh.

ItsAna:

That must be rlly hard 2 deal w.

Laur♥:

Trying 2 stay busy. But the images aren't the worst part. Tmrw is my first show @ CC. I don't want 2 be a disappointment. I've been working so hard & I don't want 2 let down my team. What if they're all expecting the LT I'm not?

Bri~xo:

They've got someone better—the LT u are now. L, u r not that rider. Ur better. Ur careful. Considerate of urself & ur horse. Tmrw's going 2 prove that.

ItsAna:

Exactly. Ur *riding* will prove that. Not whether u get a blue ribbon or no ribbon.

Laur♥:

I know I'm not the rider I was @ R. O. & I'm glad. Just worried I won't have the guts 2 ride @ all.

ItsAna:

YES, you will!!

Bri~xo:

You totally will!

Both messages came simultaneously.

Laur♥:

LOL.

ItsAna:

Double LOL.

Bri~xo:

It's gotta b true if A & I both said it.

Laur♥:

So true.☺

ItsAna:

R u having tea?

Laur♥:

U know me. *grins* I've got a cup next 2 me. Khloe made me have tea before I got online.

Bri~xo:

That makes me like her even more. Seems like a rlly good roomie.

ItsAna:

Srsly! L!! Bri got to meet her! What about me?! *pouts*

Laur♥:

Aftr the show, I'll so introduce u 2 via Skype. Promise, A! *extends pinkie*

ItsAna:

shakes pinkie ☺

Bri~xo:

What classes do u have tmrw?

Laur♥:

Trail riding & dressage.

Bri~xo:

Trail riding will b sooo fun! & dressage?? Laur, u and Wisp r going 2 do so well!

ItsAna:

Agree 100% w B. Dressage is who u r. Trail riding is going to be a class u'll heart from start to finish.

I paused in thought. My fingers hovered over the keyboard for several seconds before I wrote back.

Laur♥:

I'm excited abt trail class. But dressage is a little different. *I* have the dressage background. Whisper doesn't. We've worked SO hard & she's amazing & with time & even more work, she'll become an even better dressage horse. But she's new & young. I guess I'm afraid to push her 2 hard 2 be advanced or not to ask her for enough bc I'm afraid I can't execute certain moves the way I used to.

ItsAna:

This makes a lot of sense, L.

Bri~xo:

Thanks 4 telling us something so personal. Rlly. U already have ur test memorized 4 tmrw, right?

Laur♥:

Yep. Bc it's a schooling show, Mr. Conner gave any of us doing dressage the option of having someone call the moves, but I wanted to memorize my test like I would for any show.

ItsAna:

Wouldn't expect anything less from you. ☺ Now, go back and read what you just wrote.

What? I did what she said.

Laur♥:

Okay . . .

ItsAna:

U already have the test *memorized.* That means u've DONE it. Many, many times.

Bri~xo:

Exactly!! Thank u, Ana! See, Lauren?? There won't b any surprise moves. Nothing Wisp can't do. Nothing that u haven't done recently. U've already chosen EVERY move for the test. & if ur memory is still as crazy-sharp as it was when u were here . . . you're set. Just do the test.

I sat back against my desk chair. It had taken a long IM chat with my besties from home before the obvious had been pointed out to me. I *never* would have come to that conclusion on my own.

Laur♥:

Don't even know what 2 say. I didn't even think abt that. Not 4 a sec. Doesn't mean I'm not still scared, but it makes me feel a zillion *x a million better that I know exactly what 2 expect when I enter the arena. Thank you!!! ☺ I owe you both. Big-time.*

Bri~xo:

Don't worry. We'll collect. J So glad u feel better!! YAY!

ItsAna:

Happy 4 u, L!! U r going to enter ur classes tmrw as Lauren Towers, intermediate rider for CCA on Whisper. ☺ Doesn't that sound amaze?

Laur♥:

It rlly, rlly does. I can't thank u guys enough.

Bri~xo:

Unless u want 2 talk more, go drink ur tea & get some sleep. A & I will b thinking abt u tmrw & my phone will b glued 2 my side.

ItsAna:

Mine 2. U can do this, Laur.

Laur♥:

giant hugs Okay. Going to log off and do exactly what u said. I'll let u know how it goes!

ItsAna:

U better!! Xx

Bri~xo:

B waiting by the phone.♥

I logged off and took a big sip of tea. It felt good in my stomach, but nothing compared to what Ana and

Brielle had just told me. I had two of the best friends in the entire world, and I couldn't wait to see them. More immediately, I couldn't wait to make them proud tomorrow.

I shut off my computer, put my tea on my nightstand, and looked at Khloe. She smiled, blinking sleepily at me.

"Your friends make you feel any better?" she asked.

"So much better," I said. "I think I'm actually sleepy."

Khloe tossed her issue of *Young Rider* to the floor. "I'm so happy, Laur. You're going to be amazing tomorrow."

"Thanks, Khlo. I know you're going to shine in your classes. I can't wait to see."

We smiled at each other, double-checked our alarms, and turned off our lamps at the same time. I closed my eyes, afraid to see flashes of my accident. Instead I envisioned the first moment I saw Whisper. She'd been held by a groom, tacked up and ready for me to ride. I knew, deep down, before I'd even settled myself in the saddle, that she was special. But was she for *me*? It didn't take me long to find out.

After I'd bought Whisper, I had several conversations with Kim, my old riding instructor at Briar Creek, about her young age—she was only five—and how it was both a wonderful opportunity and a challenge. Kim had been advising me through the entire buying process, and she'd put her SOA (seal of approval) on Whisper.

Whisper was younger than most horses who competed at the level I had on the show circuit, and she hadn't had much experience in the show circuit. None at the level that Skyblue and I had reached. Kim had told me the reality that it would take years of training to make Whisper a solid event horse. She saw the same beauty that I did in the situation—I'd get to train and grow with Whisper.

Not one image of Red Oak entered my mind before I fell asleep.

23

WAKE UP!

BEEP! BEEP! BEEP! BEEP!

Ding! Ding!

Khloe and I slapped our alarm clocks and turned on our lights. There was no haze, no early morning sleepiness. I looked at Khloe and knew she felt the same way.

"Show day!" Khloe sang. She yanked back her covers and put her feet on the floor.

"Oh, my God. It's really here. We're showing. Today." I blinked at the clock. 4:02 a.m.

Khloe got up and sat at the end of my bed. I'd scrunched my legs to my chest, wrapping my arms around them.

"How are you feeling?" Khloe asked. Her brown eyes met mine. "It's okay if you're scared. More than okay. But I know you're going to be amazing, and so is Whisper."

I took a minute to reply, considering how I really *did* feel. It wasn't what I'd expected.

"I'm scared," I said. "More nervous than I've ever been before a show. Even when I went up against nationally ranked riders. At the same time, I'm excited. I get to show with Whisper, and I'm proud of everything we've done together. That makes me want to get into the arena."

"I'm sorry you're nervous," Khloe said. "I think it can act to your advantage, though, and keep you on your toes." She smiled. "I'm *really* happy that you're looking forward to your classes with Wisp. Trail is going to be a fun class and dressage, hello!"

I smiled. "Same for you. I love that we're doing the same classes even though we're not competing against each other."

"Me too. C'mon."

Khloe pulled me out of bed and, giggling, we started getting ready. After we'd taken turns washing our faces at the sink, we got dressed.

I sat on my bed to pull on my shoe boots. My Black-Berry button blinked.

I opened BBM and there were new messages.

Taylor:

Wanted 2 say good luck, Laur. (Why do these things start so early, btw?!) I know u'll be great. Tell me how it goes!!

I stared at the message for a few seconds. Then I wrote back, typing fast.

Lauren:

OMG, I can't believe u got up @ 4am 2 msg me. That was so sweet, Tay. Thank u. TTYL.

I opened the other message.

Mom & Dad:

Morning, honey. Dad and I wanted to wish you good luck again. You and Whisper are going to do so well, and we'll be thinking about you! We love you so much. Xoxo Mom and Dad

They'd called last night and left a voice mail because I was already asleep. It was nice to have their voices on my phone in case I wanted to replay the message later. I locked my phone and put it in the kangaroo pocket of my sweatshirt.

I pulled on my boots and stopped in front of the full-length mirror. Side by side, Khloe and I put our hair into low twists. Minutes later, we'd grabbed our helmets and were out the door.

Campus was *crawling* with different horses and riders. Trailers and vans filled the parking lot. Horses unfamiliar with Canterwood let out shrill neighs that elicited responses from other horses. A WELCOME banner hanging above the main entrance greeted the four schools in attendance. Mr. Conner had enlisted help from the older riders to hang the banner.

Today Canterwood was facing off against Regent Country Day, St. Agnes Academy, and Sterling Preparatory. I'd purposely not Googled the schools or looked up their riding teams. I wanted to go in not knowing the competition. In my mind, each school trained as hard as Canterwood. True or not, I didn't know.

Mike and Doug directed the guests where to go. I was so glad not to be one of them. Being on home turf comforted me more than I'd imagined.

Sunlight had started to cast a light glow over the grounds. The early October air was slightly chilly, but the forecast had called for a warmer afternoon. Mr. Conner couldn't have picked a more ideal show date if he'd tried.

Khloe and I were quiet as we went to the tack room for our gear. We hugged, and I squeezed her extra hard.

"We'll run into each other all the time," she said. "Remember, the show won't last all day. I'll try to make it to your classes, I promise. If you hear someone in the stands yelling, 'Lauren Towers is my bestie and roomie! YAY!' then you know I'm there."

I laughed. "What about if you just kept *that* to yourself?

I'd like to keep you *in* the stands and not tossed out for cheering."

Khloe grinned. "We'll see. Good luck, but you don't need it."

"You too."

We hugged again and split up.

I sidestepped horses and riders and scrambled around tack, grooming kits, and boots to get to Whisper. Schedules for today's classes were posted everywhere. My dressage class was my first, and I had a break before trail class. I could watch Khloe and Ever do dressage while I waited for my trail class to start.

"Morning, sweetie," I said, peering into her stall.

Though it was incredibly early, the mare was awake. Her eyes were wide open, and gray ears flicked back and forth at the unusually high sound level in the stable.

I entered the stall and hugged Whisper. Her coat was soft and shiny as I ran my hands along her neck. The extra grooming I'd done showed.

"You look beyond beautiful," I said. "Thank you for not lying down last night."

Whisper's gray coat was as clean as when I'd left her. Her braids were in tight knots, and the braid in her tail looked as if I'd just done it.

"We're going to stay in your stall while we get you ready," I said. "It's too busy out there."

I didn't want to take the chance of any unfamiliar horses making Whisper nervous.

"Knock, knock," a soft voice said. Lexa peeked her head into the stall, smiling at me. "Morning."

"Early enough for you?" I asked.

Lexa groaned. "Don't even mention the time, please. How are you feeling?"

"Good," I said. "I don't want to stay in the stable too long and give myself a chance to stall."

"Smart. Maybe grab a free spot in one of the arenas and warm up?"

"Exactly what I was thinking."

"I'm going to get ready too. I'm glad our dressage class is first so we can get it over with. Then we'll be able to relax and have fun with the trail class. It's so cool that we get to ride English and not Western for the class."

"I know. Otherwise, I would have taken a pleasure class."

Lexa said she'd see me at our first class and went to focus on Honor. I turned my attention back to Whisper. It didn't take long to groom her already shiny coat. I tacked her up, applied fly spray, and painted her hooves with clear polish. Phase one: complete.

24
TIME'S UP

DURING THE WARM-UP, I APPLIED THE NEW techniques Mr. Conner had taught my class this week. I ignored the swirl of black, gray, chestnut, and other colors of horses around us. All my focus was on Whisper. She was responding in return by listening to each cue. If this was *all* we did today, I'd be proud. I was *back*, and I had Whisper with me. I'd spotted Clare and Cole in another arena. I'd started to look for Riley, then I remembered.

I sat deep in the saddle, trotting her toward the arena exit. In the other, bigger arena, the obstacles for the trail course had already been set up.

In the smaller arena, dressage markers were in place. I couldn't wait to begin. Bleachers had been set up on the outside of the fence for students and riders who wanted to watch whatever class was happening in the arena. Four judges, three women and a man, readied piles of papers and pulled out chairs to sit at the banquet table that was up against the arena fence.

"Hey! Watch it!"

A horse bumped against Whisper's hindquarters.

"What are you doing?" I said, edging Whisper over. "There's plenty of room!"

A brunette on a bay tugged on her horse's reins, yanking the horse over. "Apparently, our definitions of 'room' are *seriously* different."

I wasn't going to argue with her. It wasn't worth it— I'd learned that a long time ago. I eased Whisper to a walk and let the horse and rider get well ahead of us before we followed them out of the arena.

Riders were allowed to stay in the warm-up arena, but Mr. Conner, Mike, and Doug signaled to everyone else to exit the spaces that were about to be used for show.

Classes.

Were.

Starting.

A voice I didn't recognize announced the start of the advanced show-jumping class and called for riders to report to the arena immediately.

Mr. Conner put a loudspeaker to his mouth. "May I please have all the competitors for the intermediate dressage class in the arena marked with the number three? Again, all riders for the intermediate dressage class, please report now to arena three."

I walked Whisper toward Mr. Conner, watching as a few other riders headed in the same direction. I smiled, breathing a little easier, when Lexa and Honor popped into view. We halted on the side of the entrance, and I counted ten other riders joining us.

Lexa and I didn't speak—I imagined she was focusing too.

I didn't allow myself to spend much time watching the guys and girls around me. That was something Old Lauren would have done. Canterwood Lauren stayed focused on her horse.

"Welcome, everyone," Mr. Conner said. He'd put the loudspeaker on a nearby table. "For those of you who are not Canterwood students, I'm honored to have you, your horses, and your instructors here. Each of you here has signed up for the intermediate dressage class."

I stroked Whisper's neck. My eyes caught a chestnut striking the grass with a foreleg, blowing a breath through his nostrils.

"The order has been set, and a judge will call your name when it's time for your test," Mr. Conner continued. "If you did not memorize your test, please let me know before entering the arena and I will make sure a caller is in place."

"While waiting for your turn, please feel free to walk your horse in this area." Mr. Conner waved to it with his hand. "But refrain from loud talking or cell phone use. When your name is called, please head for the arena entrance. I wish each of you the best, and it's time to begin."

Time to begin. Those words rolled around in my brain. It was *time to begin* my first show since Red Oak. No. My first show as a Canterwood Crest Academy student.

"Jenny Kai and Striker," the male judge called. A girl in a white blouse rode a liver chestnut to the entrance.

"Do you want to watch each test?" Lexa whispered. "Or walk a few steps away and get out of the crowd?"

"Let's move a little. Then we can watch and talk if we want."

Lexa and I walked Honor and Whisper to the designated waiting spot that Mr. Conner had pointed out earlier. It was within hearing distance when the judges called our names, and close enough to watch the dressage tests.

"Much better," I said. "Now I don't feel like I'm *in* the arena."

"Or feel trapped among the other riders, who are *sure* to start gossiping, I mean bashing each other, any second." Lexa rolled her eyes.

We waited, talking on and off, as riders were called into the arena for their tests. I went between watching parts of tests and talking to Lexa. Some riders exited with frowns as soon as the judges couldn't see. Some left with smiles. Others had blank expressions.

"Lexa Reed and Honor," Mr. Conner called.

I jumped in the saddle at hearing my friend's name.

"That's you!" I said. "I mean, obviously!"

Lexa laughed. "It *is* me. Okay. Wish me luck!"

"Good luck! You're going to kill it, Lex."

With a parting smile, Lexa cued Honor forward. The strawberry roan gleamed—her mix of red and white hair had been washed and brushed until not a speck of dust was left. Lexa looked like a pro in her black helmet, a brick-red blouse, black breeches, and tall boots.

She halted Honor at the entrance. I crossed my fingers, wishing her a good ride. Lexa was not my competition today. The only rider I was competing with was myself.

Lexa walked Honor to the center of the arena, halted, and

saluted the judges. As she moved through her test, gliding from marker to marker, my fingers uncrossed. Lexa didn't need luck—she was *brilliant*. Honor's circles were even, she changed gaits the second Lexa asked her to, and Lexa didn't forget one movement of the test. She stopped Honor in the center, dipped her head again, and rode out of the arena.

I walked Whisper forward so we met before Lex reached our spot.

"That was gorgeous!" I said, high-fiving her.

Grinning, Lexa patted Honor's neck. "Thanks! I think we did well for our first show of the season."

"You did more than 'well.' I'm so proud of you. Your scores will be great."

We watched the judge's table, and I squinted to see if I could read any of their facial expressions to get a hint of how Lexa had done.

Mr. Conner took a sheet of paper from the judge at the end and raised the bullhorn to his mouth.

Lexa reached out and grasped my hand. We squeezed them tight.

"The score for Lexa Reed of Canterwood Crest Academy is . . . thirty-two points!"

"Yes!" I said. "Lex! That's so low—it's awesome! You barely made any mistakes."

Lexa rubbed Honor's neck. "Good job, girl. I'm so proud of you. And thanks, LT! I'm really—"

"Next, we have Lauren Towers on Whisper!" Mr. Conner's voice boomed through the megaphone, cutting off Lexa.

"Now it's *you*," she said, smiling. "You've got this, Lauren. Go show off *your* horse!"

I stared at her. My mouth went dry. "I—I—"

Lexa locked eyes with me. "You are going to perform the test you know backward and forward. You'll be exiting the arena wishing your test was longer. I know it!"

I don't know if it was something she said, or strength from Whisper, or a combination of the two, but I smiled. A real smile.

"See you in a few," I said, taking a breath.

I squeezed my legs against Whisper's sides, and she walked toward the arena. She felt *ready*. The question was—was I?

25

IT'S ON

I PAUSED WHISPER AT THE ARENA ENTRANCE. Thoughts of scoring and points left my head. I could guide my horse, but I couldn't control her. It was our first judged test together, and however we did today, we'd do better next time. All I wanted was to enter the arena on *my* horse and give it our all.

I squeezed my legs against Whisper's sides, and we entered at a working trot. At X, the center of the arena, I brought her to a halt. She didn't stop square, but her response was immediate. I saluted the judges, and we proceeded to C at a working trot. With each stride, Whisper's body settled into the test. I wondered if she'd memorized it too.

When we reached C, she made a *parfait* twenty-meter

circle to B. Through K, X, and M, I changed rein and guided Whisper to a working trot.

She acted as if she knew what I wanted before I asked. Each movement was fluid, and there was no hesitation. I forgot about the audience. The judges disappeared. Even Mr. Conner wasn't present. It was just Whisper and me doing what I loved and what Whisper was clearly meant to do.

We moved through several more movements and reached C again. Between C and M, Whisper got to shine with a working canter on the left lead. She shook out her mane, snorting happily. It would add points to our score, but I didn't care. Whisper was enjoying herself, and it showed.

We finished the remainder of our moves—another circle, a free walk, a medium walk—and made our way back to X.

There was nothing that could keep the smile off my face. I halted Whisper and saluted the judges, beaming. Whisper and I left the arena, and I couldn't reach Lexa— and Khloe!—fast enough.

"LAUREN!" Khloe yelled.

"Shhh!" Lexa and I said, giggling.

"Omigod, that was amazing!" Khloe said, her voice

lower. "You both performed like, like—I don't even know!"

My face got hot. "Thanks, Khlo. That means a lot!"

"Seriously, Lauren," Lexa said. "You just torpedoed my score."

"Doubtful," I said. "I can say for the first time *ever* that I wasn't thinking about points the entire time. I'm *so* happy right now, because it's over! There's no 'first show after Red Oak' looming over me anymore."

Khloe and Lauren smiled.

"That must feel so good," Khloe said.

The megaphone crackled. "The score for Lauren Towers is . . . twenty-nine and a half," Mr. Conner announced.

"Told you!" Lexa said, lightly punching my arm. "I'm so happy for you!"

I couldn't believe it. Explanations about the scoring ran through my head. It was a schooling show. Judges weren't adding points as harshly.

Stop. So what if it's a schooling show and you don't know how the judges are scoring. You have a twenty-nine and a half!

I got out of my own head and stopped trying to talk myself out of counting my good score as "real."

Khloe, Lauren, and I stayed together while we waited for the remaining riders to finish. We talked, making it impossible to hear scores. And I didn't try to listen.

"I've got my break after this," I said. "And obviously, so does Lex."

"Perf!" Khloe said. "I get two cheerleaders while I do my dressage test."

"I can't wait to watch you ride," I said.

"Me either," Lexa added.

I rubbed Whisper's shoulder. "Now I'm insanely excited about our trail class later," I said to Lex. "Dressage was the one thing that was making me crazy nervous. The next class will be fun."

"The final rider for this intermediate dressage class has been given his score," Mr. Conner said from the center of the arena. "The judges are taking a final look at the individual scores to determine placement for this class."

Lexa and I looked at each other. "All I know is that you're ahead of me," Lex said. "I didn't hear another score. Did you?"

I shook my head. "Not one."

I waited for the feeling of nerves to hit. The anticipation of where I placed. The excitement or disappointment that would come with it. But my hands didn't sweat. I didn't scream at the judges in my head, wishing they'd hurry. I just waited. I was proud of my horse, and no matter what, completing my first class since my accident felt like I'd won a giant trophy.

"We have the final scores," Mr. Conner said. "If your name is called, please come into the arena for your ribbon."

Lexa, Khloe, and I held hands.

"In third place," Mr. Conner continued, "Madison Hamilton on Avery from Regent Country Day!"

Cheers and clapping broke out from the bleachers. A slight blonde on a leggy black gelding rode into the arena to await her ribbon.

"In second place," Mr. Conner said, "Lexa Reed on Honor from Canterwood Crest Academy!"

"YAY!" Khloe and I cheered.

"Omigod!" Lexa said. She grinned, looking back and forth between Khloe and me. "Yes! Omigod!"

She trotted Honor into the arena, stopping her next to Madison and Avery.

Khloe grasped my hand. "You've got this, Laur."

"We don't know that yet," I whispered.

Mr. Conner put the megaphone to his mouth again.

"And in first place . . . congratulations to Lauren Towers and Whisper from Canterwood Crest Academy!"

I didn't move. It was as if I hadn't heard Mr. Conner.

"Laur? Lauren! Omigod! You won!" Khloe shook my arm.

I looked at her. Mr. Conner's words weren't registering. Neither were Khloe's.

"You're in shock," she said. She leaned closer to me. "Lauren Towers, you won first place."

Then it hit me. All of it.

I'd shown.

There hadn't been an accident.

I'd ridden my own horse.

I hadn't let the days I missed stop me from backing out.

Leaning down, I hugged Whisper's neck, crying and laughing at the same time. I looked up and saw a rider standing in his stirrups on the other side of the arena. Drew put two fingers in his mouth and whistled. Laughing, I waved at him.

"Go! Get your ribbon!" Khloe said, laughing.

It felt like a dream as I started Whisper toward the shiny blue ribbon. It was official: Our journey on the show circuit had begun.

ABOUT THE AUTHOR

Twenty-five-year-old Jessica Burkhart (aka Jess Ashley) writes from Brooklyn, New York. She's obsessed with sparkly things, lip gloss, and listening to Lady Gaga. She loves hanging with her bestie, watching too much TV, and purse shopping. Learn more about Jess at JessicaBurkhart.com. Find everything Canterwood Crest at CanterwoodCrest.com.